Amaranth Bower

Luke Winterborne

Basinghall Books
London

ISBN: 978-0-615-93050-3

Printed in the United Kingdom

Bereavement

Eternity points, in its amaranth bower
Where no clouds of fate o'er the sweet prospect lour,
Unspeakable pleasure, of goodness the dower,
When woe fades away like the mist of the heath.

Percy Bysshe Shelley

Part One

I

Wearing the old bathrobe Alec tried unsuccessfully to throw away last summer, Kirsten stood at the breakfast nook window. The quiet house breathed lilac scent from flowers placed beside a family portrait. Their scent filled the rooms. She stood a long while in the kitchen simply looking at the pre-dawn sky, and the undulating curves of the Mancunian Way, not quite a motorway, not really a way to anywhere, but a lovely friend all the same. Looking up, the pink-tinted morning clouds startled her. Funny, she thought, how rarely she looked at the sky. Alec noticed things like the sky, he often commented on stars and planes he saw. 'I saw an A380,' he'd say. Kirsten had nothing like those powers of observation. What did she observe? Handsome men, the time of day things happened, Alec's moods. Could that be the entirety of her list? Surely she noticed more things? Although 3:35 in the morning, noise from the perpetually busy street below their embankment insinuated its way up to her. Their Siamese cat *the cat* huddled the warmth on the sofa where she'd been sitting. His eyes were open, as he considered asking her for a meal.

Pressed open against the spine, a book on the coffee table grew a fur of dust. On the window-ledge another family photograph looked at her and she turned it over, face down, and then tears dropped along her cheek, a weakness hidden even from the photographically imprisoned souls of her family. In her hand she held George's obituary. Mom had sent it to her, clipped from the local paper, not yet yellowed. Across the top, like a Blake poem, the words 'Little Boy drowned' leapt out. Her hand had sweated a blur over the letters. Size alone showed that this boy's life hardly signified, in the grander newspaper scheme of things. She turned back to the cat, crumpled up the obituary, threw it into the trash.

"I can't keep reading it, can I?" she said.

The cat mewed dutifully.

Kirsten tried to imagine George as a drowned body. She only recalled a living, blond-haired boy at his fourth birthday party. And Brooke? Had Brooke even begun to forgive Julian? When young, Brooke and Julian were closest, always hatching conspiracies against Kirsten. Once, on an Arizona camping trip, they zipped Kirsten out of the tent when she went to the bathroom. She cut her nose on the massive zipper trying to get back in as the other two siblings giggled in their sleeping bags. Brooke would never have considered Julian untrustworthy, Julian would have been the last person she'd think would abandon George to wander up the breakwater and drown. Julian had always been every mother's son, the perfect child, handsome, smart, envied ... an all American gay, because he carried that off with bare-chested gay aplomb as brilliantly as he did everything else.

The last time Brooke and Kirsten talked neither of them mentioned the accident, and they never mentioned Julian. But Brooke must know he planned to stay with them this summer. What did she think about that? Kirsten pressed her face into the lilacs, the vase itself a birthday gift from Brooke. Instead of the flowers she smelled Brooke's kitchen in Santa Monica, garlic, freshly peeled and pressed, dripping aromatically, sizzling oil, with the tangy-fresh fragrance of basil. People marveled over Brooke's kitchen; the lifestyle section of the paper featured her once, because, although a busy young mother, she made her own flavored pastas and stuffed her ravioli herself.

The cat watched Kirsten curiously, Siamese ears alert.

Then Kirsten closed her eyes and leaned against the breakfast bar. She felt George there with her, an illusion so real that his breath tickled her arm and his hair brushed against her fingers. Last Christmas, during Kirsten and Alec's visit, she and Brooke went to The Grove in Los Angeles and shopped in the after Christmas sales. George celebrated his fourth birthday party during that trip. Brooke threw the party because she knew that Alec and Kirsten – who spaced their Californian trips out carefully – wouldn't be there for his fifth. How fateful, Kirsten thought. She and Brooke were never closer than on that trip to the mall. Kirsten observed a lot that day: Brooke's smiles, the peculiar December heat, the guards in the parking lot, a bossy sales lady, a used condom in the bushes.

Brooke said, "That's a weird place for a condom."

Kirsten replied, 'I've seen them in weirder places.'

Brooke said 'like where?'

Kirsten said, 'like in my hair one morning.'

Brooke shrieked with laughter. Was your hair really a weird place to find a condom after a night of youthful frolicking? Something sad emanated from Brooke even then, Kirsten thought, a penumbra of death clung to her a full six months before George drowned. Kirsten looked up at the clock over her sink. Then she went to the phone and dialed the number. It had just gone eight o'clock at night in California. "Chris, it's me," she said when Brooke answered. And then, quickly, to hide an unexpected

11

nervousness which crept up on her, "I'm standing here drinking a cup of coffee and thinking about you."

"Hang on," Brooke said, "it's only, what, four in the morning there?"

"I couldn't sleep."

"Something bothering you?"

"No. How's Wyatt?"

"He's okay," Brooke said.

Her listless words hung fire.

Kirsten waited, until she realized she waited for nothing. "Is he, well, you know?"

"Do I know *what*?"

"Is he back at work?"

"Sort of."

"Part time, you mean?"

"Whatever."

"And you?" Kirsten asked.

"Women are stronger, aren't they?"

"I've never thought so."

"I've had cause to think about it."

"I guess so," Kirsten said.

"This sleepless coffee drinking wouldn't have anything to do with Julian's upcoming visit would it?"

"He arrives this morning."

"You didn't answer my question," Brooke said.

Kirsten tried to conjure up a telepathic image of her sister. What did she wear, where did she sit? She imagined a pink blouse, jeans, white socks, designer shoes, the ones Brooke called her Connecticut shoes. Probably she sat in the living room, watching TV, only she turned it off when she answered the phone and heard Kirsten's voice. This image comforted.

"Yes," Kirsten said, "it has to do with his visit."

"Don't you want him there? If not, you should have told him. He seems to think he's as welcome as sunshine."

"Why? What did he say?" Kirsten asked.

"Nothing to me directly. I'm repeating what mom tells me."

"What'd mom say he said?"

"You know, Kirsten, tonight – I hyperventilated when I was listening to Lady Gaga. Remember that song *Alejandro?*"

"Hyperventilated?" Kirsten couldn't even remember what that meant. Breathing too fast? She adjusted her gears. "I'm sorry. I don't know Lady Gaga's songs that well."

"I was wheezing like an asthmatic. Wyatt went rushing for the Xanax."

Kirsten stayed quiet. She couldn't think what to say about Brooke wheezing over a Lady Gaga song.

"But, I mean," Brooke said, "it was good that I had a reaction."

"Good?"

"Yes. It's been hard for me to react, but my shrink keeps telling me how important it is, so she'll be pleased. She puts names to what I'm going through, you see, denial, sublimation. Everything we feel conveniently has a name, did you know that?"

"I suppose."

"Is it hard for you to talk about this, Kirsten?"

"I'm afraid of saying the wrong thing ... or something."

"It's all right. There's no right or wrong thing. You can even say his name. I can say his name. George. There. See. I said it."

"George," Kirsten said.

"There."

"I'm sorry if I don't handle it well, talking to you and all. I try."

"People try," Brooke said. "That's the important thing. That they try. Because nobody really knows how to deal with parents who've lost a child." She didn't say 'in an accident.' Kirsten noted the omission. "Don't be nervous about Julian's visit," Brooke said "The visit itself will probably be uneventful. As far as Julian is concerned he'll sit around and agonize and feel sorry for himself. That's what he does. Personally? I wish he'd get hit by a bus on the first day in Manchester ... do they have those double-deckers there? ... And his head would explode like that pumpkin we blew up with a cherry bomb. Remember? That time at Grandpa and Grandma Hathaway's house?"

Brooke's words stunned Kirsten into silence. She stared at her drapes, admiring the velvet and the folds, as if somehow the mystery to their upended lives might be found in draperies. Seconds crept by. She knew she should say something. "I shouldn't have called like this," she finally got out. She hadn't meant to say that. But she did.

"Look. You're justifiably uncomfortable about his visit, I understand that."

"What'd mom say he said about coming over here?"

"That you'd understand him, that you'd help him," Brooke said. "You're always trying to help people, aren't you, Kirsten? It makes you feel needed. Being needed makes you feel loved."

"*Excuse me*? Suffering aside, Chris, you've no right to ... well, you make me sound like a psychological cripple." She noticed that as her voice rose, she began again to examine the curtains. Why?

"I have no rights and no ... whatever ... okay. I'm just going to say whatever the fuck I want to say and when I hit your button, go ahead and hang up."

A longer, uglier, meaner silence grew between them; the silence of sisters who'd never really got along. Why should they know? This time Kirsten rejected the drapes and sitting smack in the middle of the floor, with Bête Laide immediately in her lap, she closed her eyes in order to concentrate. "I was thinking about our trip to the mall at Christmas," Kirsten told her. "Do you remember how we found that condom in the bushes? I was thinking about how close we were that day. Listen, why don't you and Wyatt come over?"

"While Julian is there? He's planning on staying for six months. When do you want us? For Christmas? We can come the day after he leaves?"

"*Oh*," Kirsten said. "I wasn't thinking." So much for closed-eye lotus position. She stood up abruptly, causing poor Bête Laide to sprawl over the sofa.

"I suppose we might be up to coming next summer. We could think about that."

"Alec always enjoys Wyatt's company."

Another awkward quiet gripped the line.

"I'm glad you told me about hyperventilating over that song, I mean I'm glad you could share that," Kirsten said. "I'm bad about calling. I will call more often," Kirsten said.

"Oh, boy ... thrills and *chills* ... Julian can sit there and listen. Fun all round."

"You really hate him," Kirsten said.

"Hate's a mild word for what I feel for him."

"He's your brother."

"Think again," Brooke said. "Husbands and wives divorce each other. Well, brothers and sisters can divorce each other too. Let's consider that I've divorced him. He's no longer my brother, he's this shithead who killed my baby and got away with it." Her voice hit shrill high notes of despair. "They should have ... what? Hell, I don't know. Gassed him at San Quentin or stoned him to death in the middle of the fucking street."

Oh, my dear God, Kirsten thought. Why did I call? What vein of emotion have I opened here? "*Brooke.*"

"*Kirsten,*" Brooke said back sarcastically.

"Julian was neglectful maybe, or distracted ... but he didn't murder George, you know that. George ran away from him and then he fell from the breakwater and drowned."

"He killed him all right."

Brooke had grown so strong that she'd become a stone, Kirsten thought. Once again the line fell quiet, tingling with snowfall static. "I'm glad you're seeing a psychiatrist. I'm so sorry, Chris. About George, I mean. You know I am."

"Yes," Brooke said. "I know you are."

"I'd better go," Kirsten said.

"I know I'm prickly," Brooke said suddenly, and a change came into her voice, something which reminded Kirsten uncannily of their Aunt Meredith. None of them had ever liked Aunt Meredith, they found her hard. According to their Uncle Alvin, who recounted the story behind Aunt Meredith's back, she once threw all of her Christmas cards in the trash saying, 'I hate getting these goddamned fake things.' "Really," Brooke said, "I'm glad you called."

"My love to Wyatt."

"And mine to Alec."

This woman's heart has broken, Kirsten thought, and she no longer recognized Brooke as the

16

sister with whom she grew up. Where had the Brooke gone who practiced with her pompoms and gorgeous, big-boobed A-list friends in the garage? Where was the Brooke who sang like Melissa Etheridge in the shower? Kirsten saw that those Brookes were lost forever and that wherever this new Brooke was, Kirsten would never again know her.

"Bye," Kirsten said.

"Bye," Brooke said back.

Julian gazed at the Palm trees on Ocean Avenue. When his look returned to the therapist's waiting room, he saw he'd picked a scab off his elbow. Blood oozed from the wound. With his little finger he touched a drop, held it up, and wiped it off on his sock. DNA, he thought, courtroom drama, 'unlikely,' said the attorney, 'that the accused would wipe his *own* blood on the sock.' He leapt up, grabbed his coat from the coat rack, plunged into the parking lot, and ran across the street to a shopping mall, through a bank of doors and up a staircase. At the top of the stairs he stood winded, confused, as if expecting the stairs to keep on going, to stretch through the roof into the clouds. He looked on the tiered levels of the shopping mall. Some of the shops resembled Dickensian storefronts; others had grinning sunbursts, neon lights, and imitation burled wood, a happy kangaroo in a hat and maroon jump-suit. Because his hands trembled he grasped the rail.

Though he tried to calm himself, he grew aware, seeing his reflection in a luggage store window, that he looked outlandish, too skinny for his clothes, a pale man with protruding bones and shadows under luminous eyes. He pulled his phone from his pocket and with surprising memory called to his sister Kirsten in Manchester.

"Kirsten, I'm in a mall," he said when she picked up the phone.

"Julian?"

"A shopping mall."

"What?"

"I'm not at work today. I can see some luggage here. You know I don't have a decent suitcase ... not even one."

Silence. Then, *"Julian? What's happened? What's the matter?"*

Silence.

"Call mom," Kirsten said.

Silence.

"Julian? Are you still there? Call mom. She'll come get you."

Silence.

He touched the *terminer* bar on his phone – he had programmed his phone entirely in French, for reasons no long forgotten – and walked into the luggage store, where a salesman – seemingly startled by his haggard appearance – moved toward him. Forcing his voice into his best teacher mode, Julian said, "May I see something in green please?"

"Green? Do you have ... well, a size in mind?"

"Big. A big green suitcase with those swiveler wheels so that you can make it twirl."

After staring at Julian as if he thought his best option might be summoning security, he opted for making a sale. So Julian bought a green, leather-trimmed twirler suitcase and took it with him to the food court, where he ordered a double tall mocha with no whipped cream and sat at a window looking out on a peaceful street in Santa Monica.

"You got nice dimples," said a woman, who nosed her way through the automatic doors with a stolen shopping cart full of her belongings, warily watching for security guards.

"Thanks."

He watched his hands twitch on the table top, and as he thought of the guest room in Kirsten and Alec's house in Didsbury, a leafy Manchester suburb, with the radiator upon which he dried his socks, and suddenly he felt drowsy and his hands stopped twitching. He could sleep again in England."

"I need five bucks," the homeless lady said.

They stared at each other a moment, and then Julian took twenty dollars for his wallet, wadded it up and threw it on the ground.

"Retard," she said.

He picked up the bag and clutched it to his chest, a talisman, and he heard his first whisper of freedom and with that whisper came the phone number for school and the memory of his therapist's appointment.

Kirsten lay in frothy bath water. She bathed now in the mornings, since they didn't expect her at work until nine and she often squeezed that out until nine thirty without anyone complaining. At the moment she thought about her two phone calls last night from her brother Julian, one from a mall and one from his apartment, saying that he planned to come to Paris to visit – and stay for six months.

Her husband Alec squinted into the accordion mirror over the sink as he shaved. They met fifteen years ago, when Kirsten, a University of California exchange student, attended a party in a block of student flats belonging to Manchester University. She thought Alec had exhaled sensuality, in his moth eaten sweater, white shirt, jeans and shaggy hair. Subtle inquiries revealed he worked on a dissertation about Lord Byron's politics. She introduced herself to him, he asked her out. On their third date he looked at her and said, "With all that dark hair, you make me believe that one woman, at least, walks in beauty like the night." They went home and made love. Tommy Webster, Kirsten's high school boyfriend back home, never stood a chance. She wrote his 'Dear Tommy' letter the next morning.

"Society still commodifies women, doesn't it?" Alec continued with their conversation. They often had their best conversations while one or the other of them bathed. "Their beauty is their value. Something like that. All women go through a phase like this."

"I disagree," she said, "not with that commodifying stuff, I actually agree with that. I mean, I think this is my problem. I don't want it to be a phase, that's patronizing, and it's not something you can dismiss by saying 'all women go through this.'"

"But I should think you'd like the feminist argument. Solidarity. *Epater* the patriarchy."

He provided no help with her confused self-image. "I'm not into feminist solidarity anymore, I'm into feminist *individuality*." She thought that an embarrassing thing to have said, so she muttered, "oh well," returning to their earlier discussion, the one they had conducted in bed that morning, "Anyway, it's not Julian's fault." She must have said those words a hundred times now. "That's the thing."

"No," Alec said. "That's not the thing."

She looked at him again but discerned no expression on his face. Their cultural differences had long ago evaporated, yet at times something English popped up, encoded in his DNA. He could be a sphinx, this boy from sophisticated commuter belt London, who grew up playing soccer, cricket and rugby and rowed competitively. Kirsten, from Santa Monica, never played sports of any kind. She thought about telling him he looked cute in his new boxer shorts, which he did, however she thought he didn't deserve a compliment this morning. "Why'd you say 'that's not the thing?'" she asked.

"Because it isn't. It was his fault. He had his priorities wrong, didn't he? If he'd been attentive it wouldn't have happened."

She slipped deeper into the raspberry-scented suds. Alec had made it clear that he thought it odd – at best – that a thirty year old man would quit his job and come to England for six months. That hardly jibed with Alec's view of the world. Considering the depth of Julian's distress, Kirsten didn't think it odd that he come to France. Equally she wouldn't think it odd if he were institutionalized and administered electro-convulsive therapy.

Alec finished shaving and rinsed his face.

"It's awkward, Kirsten."

"Awkward?"

"Awkward for me. I have strong feelings about Julian's behavior."

She didn't know what to say about it being awkward for Alec.

He sat on the edge of the tub. "Can he be encouraged to travel the continent or something?

21

Maybe we can give him the keys to Margot and Philippe's place in the Vendee."

"Alec. Stop it."

"He'd love the Vendee."

"Why should he love it there?" she asked.

"You're being unkind."

"My, how *English* my beautiful wife has become. I'm being *unkind*? I remember when the word *du jour* would have been asshole." He splashed a little water on her face. "I've never minded his visits before, have I?"

"He's never stayed longer than two weeks before. You could endure Attila the Hun for two weeks."

"Wrong," he said. "You know full well I climb the walls if my sister stays longer than two days."

"I invited him."

"You didn't. He asked."

She stared into his face. "What's the real problem, Alec?"

"I'm angry." Alec stood up. "I'm a probable father someday. Quite frankly, I blame him. I'm sorry, but there we are, my sympathies ... well, they lie elsewhere."

"I know where your sympathies lie." She sank beneath the water so that her hair floated around her head like a pre-Raphaelite Ophelia. She slurped back up and said, "Julian has been through hell. Utter hell."

"Right, utter hell."

"I recognize that tone of voice."

"That's another reason why I love you, darling ... in addition to knock-out good looks, you're so clever." He toweled his hair further and left the bathroom.

She heard his feet clomp across the hall to their bedroom. Her own toes wiggled at her from next to the hot water tap. Alec's argument made sense, she understood his feelings, and then again, Julian had suffered torment. In their conversations Kirsten heard his bleakness, detected his despair. She felt sorry for him, he *had* been through hell. Alec or no Alec she'd make him feel welcome, help him face the future. This made her feel better. She stood up, grabbed the towel and rubbed her skin vigorously.

Alec whistled now in the bedroom, a good sign.

"I'm going to make him welcome," she yelled. "And I expect you to be on best behavior."

"For six months?"

"Longer if necessary ... he can stay the whole year if he wants." She left the bathroom and went into the bedroom. He kissed her, she kissed him back. "My heart goes out to Julian."   "I know it does." He finished dressing and put on his raincoat. "I'll ring you this afternoon."

She accepted his final kiss. "Bye."

"Cheer up," he said, going to the door. "We'll make the best of his visit."

"Sure."

2

Julian sat upright from out of a nightmare, got out of bed and sat on his chair. Outside the window, lights played and buildings swayed, with the indiscernible shivering of the earth. Wind blew through palm fronds, homeless men dug in dumpsters, and birds, birds flew. Seagulls. Never the waves, never the ocean. He cringed from the gulls, as he smelled the salt water, heard the waves crash against the breakwater like they did that afternoon. The crash of those waves like the wreak of titanic ships, heavy with their cargo of guilt. The booming of waves, lifeguards, ambulances, harbor patrol, screams, his own screams, 'come back, George, come back.' And here nothing, here tomb-silence, until the pounding began on his door.

He went out to the living room and answered it.

"Jesus fucking Christ man, what's going on in here?"

Julian stared at his upstairs neighbor, clad only in boxer shorts, hair standing straight up, eyes bleary. Julian had always thought was cute, boyfriend potential even, and here he stood hairy-chested and masculinely rumpled and Julian felt ... *nothing*.

"It's fucking four in the morning," the neighbor said.

Nothing Julian could say to that.

"You fucking murder someone in here?"

"No. No it was a dream. I mean I had a dream," Julian said, which sounded like Martin Luther King, Jr., not like a nightmare, so he added, "a nightmare."

Stares, eyeball to eyeball.

"Fucking loony-bin man. Fucking loony bin.

You look like a friggin' scarecrow and you're fucking screaming at five in the morning. You belong in the loony bin, dude. You know?"

"Yes," Julian said, shutting the door. "I know."

Julian's grief was all-encompassing, vertical and not horizontal. There was no room in this vertical grief for other people, politeness aside. It was a grief which prompted him to come back to the breakwater before leaving tomorrow for England, and one which prompted him to walk along the edge of this painfully phosphorescent sea, but not one which allowed him to do much else. He started walking again. Where he walked, the line between dry and wet sand was indistinct. Sometimes water swirled round Julian's feet; sometimes the sand where he walked was firm and dry. Waves boomed. Froth hissed. The night closed over the sea. He looked into the void and emptiness stared back at him. Julian brought his hands up to his temples and held them there tightly. He thought this beach walking seemed mannered, like play-acting. His eyes filled with tears. Above him there were many stars, and through his tears the stars refracted as if in a prism, glints of color sparking across his night sky, and then the night covered them as well.

The salty air was warm, and his tears were warm, this warm night felt safe for anger. Tears gave his anger validity. Julian picked up a beer bottle and tossed it into the sand. It landed gently. Then he sat down in the froth, rested his chin on his hand and observed the dark Pacific Ocean. The seat of his jeans sogged with water. Then, he stood up, walked behind the snack pavilions, along the broken concrete walkway and out on the breakwater. Near the end, harder waves thundered. Julian simply stood there. Then he took off his shirt. Moonlight struck his bare chest, and he saw himself for a moment as a handsome shirtless gay man at the end of a breakwater. *"I'm still alive,"* he said to the murderous waves. He closed his eyes. He felt as if he flew, felt as if he soared up to the height of the cliffs and back again. He opened his eyes, wadded his shirt up and hurled it into the sea.

Julian awoke as the film ended. His mouth had a metallic taste, his headphones had disarranged themselves on the top of his head. He could barely open his eyes, his contacts were dried out. He reached up, snatched the phones off, crammed them into the seat pocket, and went to the toilet. A line hadn't formed yet. In the bathroom he scrubbed his face, dried it on paper towels, then took the bottle of moisturizer from his pocket and spread it over his face, under his eyes, up over his forehead. Refreshed, he returned to his seat. People moved around now. Having flown this flight to Paris before Julian knew how to pace himself. He picked up the flight magazine, flipped through it, put it back. They should serve breakfast soon, which would be a diversion. Opening his travel case he took out the novel he'd been reading, but his eyes only skimmed the page, continually returning to the same spot, so he finally gave up and put it away.

The local newspaper printed an article, probably one in twenty people read it, but Julian read it. 'Rumored to be despondent,' the article said, 'no charges to be brought.' They put in George's photograph. Did Brooke give it to them? Why put in that photograph, from George's fourth birthday party, with blond ringlets and a wicked little smile. How could anyone reading that article, seeing that face, not believe Julian a murderer? How could they not see him as a criminal? Hadn't he called himself exactly that to Wyatt and Brooke? 'I'm a criminal,' he said. Wyatt wouldn't even talk to him, Brooke gave him steely looks. He could hardly recall now the time when he and Brooke were best friends. Even his mother, in the first blush of emotion, asked, 'why'd you leave him alone, Julian? *Why?*'

He didn't know why. Because a jellyfish stung a lady and she asked Julian to help her. Because he thought George still clung to his swimsuit. He didn't know why. He knew Kirsten would have the guest room ready for him – he almost felt the duvet, remembered the floral curtains affectionately, the radiator on which he dried his socks and underwear. He leaned his head against the window. How long could he go on like this, with only mirages of radiators and floral curtains for succor? He accepted his breakfast tray from the flight attendant but faced with the food he couldn't eat. Odd, he thought, how he used to relish eating. Food once counted as a passion. Now, though he concentrated on every bite, he only swallowed a corner off the hard-crusted little omelette and drank the mineral water. The lady next to him asked for his Danish and he gave it to her.

He'd managed to get this far, but how far was it?

Julian came off the plane exhausted, as if the world had wrapped itself in gauze, and followed the signs toward immigration. As a matter of principle he avoided moving walkways, a hard walk a way of exercising after ten sedentary hours. However, on this occasion, he had a more complex motive. Definitely not in a hurry, he plopped on the treads and crawled along at a snail's pace, past advertisements for products he didn't recognize or want. But in the end, moving walkway or no moving walkway, he come to the arrivals hall, and though he paused for a moment to find a place in the longest queue, his turn came quickly, and the immigration officer stamped his passport. When he came up to the carousel with luggage from his flight, his suitcases already wheeled around. He plucked them up, carried them with him through the green channel -- for only a moment dithering, trying to think of anything he could declare -- and then out to the main terminal.

Kirsten stood sentinel. They looked at one another, then they rushed into their outstretched arms.

"Julian," Kirsten said. In her mind she had intended to shriek, as if with joy, but somehow she spoke his name almost coldly, like a statement of fact.

"Hi, Kirsten," he said, in precisely the same tone of a voice.

For a moment they were silent.

"It's so good to see you," she told him. And it did feel good to see him. In that moment all seemed pure, these were siblings reunited. They hugged more. "How was the flight?" she asked.

He shrugged. Skinnier than she anticipated, he resembled a stick-figure caricature of himself, with hollow eyes and a dead, gray look in his face.

"Did you sleep any?" she asked, which seemed an odd greeting, she wasn't sure why she asked it. Perhaps because he looked as if he hadn't slept ... in months.

"No."

"You don't mind taking the train, I hope?"

"What train?"

"Home from the airport. We're so close to Didsbury station," she said, "it seemed silly to bring the car out."

"Of course I don't mind. Why would I mind?"

Her eyes drifted toward the enormous plate glass windows at the front of the terminal. A bus went by filled with Japanese tourists, their faces at their own windows looking back in at her.

"How's Alec?" Julian asked.

"He's well," Kirsten said. "Working hard."

"As always."

"Yes. We'll ring mom, let her know you arrived safely."

"Why? She'll have heard if there were any plane crashes. Brooke will be glued to the TV and sprint over there with glee. 'He's dead, he's dead, hurrah for the terrorists.'"

Kirsten stared at him as if he'd belched. She thought of absolutely no response, she simply gaped. And so it began, she thought, and the moment's brief purity passed into oblivion and it no longer felt like a joyful reunion of siblings. She thought about her confusing conversation that morning with Brooke, balancing it in her mind with this exchange with Julian. It seemed conniving of her to listen like this to both sides of the drama, but no middle ground came into sight. She must choose sides ultimately. She didn't want to choose sides. Her head started to ache. Alec had been right, this was a mistake. It was bound to end up with her struggling irreconcilably between Brooke and Alec and Julian. Her mouth felt dry, like the morning after taking a sleeping pill. Julian watched her, she guessed he saw her befuddlement, yet he could offer nothing, too weak to alleviate anyone else's discomfort. This must be what living through the months after you led a child to his death in the sea felt like, she thought suddenly. But the unkindness of the thought made her nearly hallucinate, she grew wild with bewilderment and grief.

Then she forced herself to smile and her composure returned. "The train?" she asked.

"Which way?"

"This way." She pointed at the overhead signs. "It's a new walkway since I was here last, very modern."

"I'm impressed."

"She doesn't hate you, Julian," Kirsten said, even though Brooke had told her bluntly that she did hate him. Kirsten spoke slowly, as if the deliberateness of her words invested them with their meaning. "She's still grieving, you see. And you need to go easy. Okay?"

"Grief," he said. "Grief is something I understand." His eyes gripped her. "Because I'm still grieving too, Kirsten."

"It's not your fault," she said.

"What's not my fault?"

She fell mute.

"*What's* not my fault?" he pursued.

She felt brutalized by the question.

"Can't you say it? Or don't you believe it?"

"*Was* it your fault?" she asked. It was not what she meant to ask. She couldn't believe she asked it. It had asked itself.

"Yes."

She thought she might faint. "Don't," she managed to whisper, but whether to him or to herself was unclear. Looking at her reflection she saw the color drained from her face, lips like Morticia Addams.

"We'd better not miss the train, Kirsten." He heaved his suitcases forward.

"You can't miss it." Her voice fluttered leafily." They run every twenty minutes at least."

He looked at her; she looked back.

"Wonderful," he said, and she noticed that unlike her his color had come up, the pallor gone. Anger? "Good to know there's something in life I can't miss."

"It's not your fault," she repeated.

"Of course it is," he said, so matter of factly that it startled her, like a slap, a further victimization. "You know it is. Everyone knows it is." He pointed. "That way you said?"

3

"The language is Esperanto, don't ridicule what you don't understand," Annabella said. "It's a pluralingual cultural magazine, there's a smashing piece of erotica here in Dutch."

"You don't read Dutch."

"I can pick out the dirty bits."

"Oh that's thrilling, that is," Rutger said.

"It's all a matter of perspective, isn't it?"

She held her springy masses of hair away from her face and peered at him through a hairy frame. Annabella looked younger than thirty. Rutger, half way through being twenty-eight, looked his age.

"What's eating you then?" Annabella said.

"Nothing."

She looked incredulous.

Rutger worked the cash register, Annabella leaned over the railing. Thus perched, she looked down on the women's department and Gerard, the manager who, rumor had it, resented Rutger's good looks, never surprised them. Annabella even positioned a mirror at the top of the stairs, which allowed them to look right into his office. She was good fun. Things weren't half so lively when Pierre worked the afternoons or when Zéphyrine came up, he and Annabella were the best combination. Mind you, Rutger thought, he never imagined himself as a sales clerk in a clothing store. But here he stood, the son of parents who hoped he might be a doctor or lawyer.

"I'm a tribute to failed ambition," he said out loud.

That took her back. "So how are you a failure?" she asked.

"I didn't say I was a failure, I said I was a tribute to failed ambition. My dad's ambition."

"How so?"

"My dad had big dreams for us. I should have been a barrister or a physician. Right? I should absolutely have gone to university." He looked at her with what might pass for a smile, knowing she already knew the story. Rutger wanted to play rugby, so he played rugby. Then, at nineteen, he had a good whack, and the doctor told him not to play again, that was that. He never went to university, he had only mediocre results on entrance examinations – and now he worked in a clothing store. "I should move out to Canada. I have some long lost family out there somewhere. They struggled to get there too, ironic like. In the days when it was sails and hardship. Astrolabes and constellations, all that. So much struggle, if you think about it."

"Astro-whats?"

"What they used to navigate. But then life's like that, isn't? Twisty-turny. Ironic, very ironic. Good turns out to be bad and bad turns out to be good."

"That's Zen." Annabella watched him a moment. "You should go out more," she said.

"I do go out."

"I never see you."

"Then, Einstein, we must go to different places," he said.

A customer came up to pay for a tie. Rutger went through the procedure by rote. Why would anyone buy this thing, he wondered, an unattractive beige with green diamonds? No accounting for taste, for sure. He smiled through the carte bleue routine and folding the tie into a bag. Hardly brain work, he thought.

"You made that face," Annabella told him. "The one I told you about," she said. "The smelling sulfur face. You've got to watch that, Rugs. You won't be a manager with that face. Cringy little ass-licker Mohammed would tell Gerard, you know that. If he saw that face he'd be sure to tell Gerard."

"How do you know he hasn't already seen it and told?" Rutger asked.

"Because Zéphyrine would tell me. She hears everything downstairs." She looked at her watch. "It's nearly lunch. Here," she handed him the folded over magazine. "It's got great stories. Read them. You'll cheer up."

"This is the ... whatever you called it?"

"Pluralingual cultural magazine. You can ignore the stories in languages you don't know."

"You insist on thinking I need cheering up," he said.

"You need cheering up all right."

"I don't need this pluralingual thing, it'll make me scream."

"Primal therapy. Great." She ran to the head of the stairs and then looked at him. "You need a good woman, Rutger van der Merwe, that's what you need."

"I have a good woman," he said.

"Oy. Where've you been hiding her, then?"

"My mum. That's who she is." A stupid thing to say and he regretted it immediately.

Their eyes met from where she stood on the top stair.

"Get off, you're the Joker," she said and she laughed as she bounded down the stairs.

The meaning of life receded just when you thought you had it in your grasp, Rutger found himself thinking. He felt like he always chased the solution, which meant, he thought, that he'd never find the solution. Wonderful. An odd word to use -- solution -- he wondered what he meant by that? The woman behind him coughed continually. The brim full 96 bus careened through north Manchester. An occasional sign advertised an apartment for sale or announced some long overdue urban renewal project. A pack of skinny dogs stopped for the bus to pass. Those kinds of dogs knew how to watch out for traffic, Rutger thought, only beloved collies frisking in suburban gardens got nailed by buses on the Bury New Road. You saw their collared, fluffy corpses with bloodied mouths in front of someone's Lady Helena roses on a Saturday afternoon. The driver took corners purposefully fast and people leaned to one side in unison, their heads nearly touching, like a Monty Python skit. Why not? The driver had just this *one* opportunity to exercise control over his world. If he drove the bus, Rutger figured he'd go round corners even faster. Getting off at The Maunder Centre, he picked up a newspaper at W.H. Smith's, reading it over a cup of tea.

When the girl behind the counter smiled at him, he smiled back, but warily, distinctly alert. He'd spent his life being alert, as if getting ready to confront something. Rutger never came off his guard, his life overshadowed by the tension his alertness caused. He lived as if he were going to have to defend himself from attack. But who would attack him? And why? What frightened him so deeply? Although unsure of the precise definition of anxiety, he thought he must be anxious. Feeling like a clock spring wound ever tighter frustrated him; he couldn't fathom it. Why did he burn like an underground coal fire, never extinguished, full of an incipient power to incinerate the earth itself? The effects of his anxiety were unpredictable, mutable, ranging from accelerated heart rate, to sweaty palms, to unthinking rage. Though unnecessary, he gathered up his things and took them to the serving counter.

"Are you a teacher?" the girl asked. She pointed at the paper on the table behind him.

"No, I just like to read it."

"What do you do then?"

"I sell clothes."

"Oh," she said, visibly disappointed. "Well, it's not so bad, is it? I bet you sell a lot of them."

"It's completely fucked, if you want to know the truth. Which you probably don't," he said.

"Don't what?"

"Want to know the truth."

"It's a job, isn't it?" she said.

"Yeah," he said, "It's a job."

He nodded at her. She nodded back.

He walked down the stairs and went into Boots. There was no call to be rude, she hadn't done anything to him except smile; hardly an invitation to be insulted. He felt low, found a greeting card, though he hadn't been looking for one, paid for it and left. Crowds filled the streets; the store already stood open. Gerard smiled broadly at him as he came in, a full ten minutes early. Ignoring him, Rutger went upstairs, took the card out, and signed it.

"Here," he said to Annabella as she came up the stairs.

"What's this then?"

"A card."

37

She opened it and read it. "Why'd you buy me a card, Rutger?"

"Because I wanted to."

She read it again. "But that's amazing that is."

They stared at one another a long, warm, assessing series of encapsulated moments of understanding.

"Well," she said. "Thank you."

He shrugged; she watched him.

"What are you looking at?" he asked her.

"You."

"There's a customer."

She read the card one more time. "And am I a friend then?"

"The best."

She smiled at him and went toward the customer.

So why wasn't he happy? When he'd just given his friend a card and perked up her day? What troubled him? He looked at himself in the mirror next to the cash register. Crisp white shirt, blue and white patterned tie, braided leather belt, fashionable haircut, and charcoal gray trousers. He heard the words of the girl in the food court, reverberating like magic, a rabbit pulled from someone's knickers, 'are you a teacher?'

A teacher.

He began to understand what troubled him.

Rutger van der Merwe reminded Annabella of a broken mirror, sharp reflective pieces and dull unseeing pieces all mixed together, diffuse, scattered, a bit here, a bit there. He puzzled her. One of a large and largely unruly clan of girls she'd grown into a keen observer of human drama with a finely honed intuition. Often she thought about Rutger, without a doubt her best friend, a good man, a person whom she trusted. And she thought she knew his problem. When the right time appeared, she'd tell him so too, because as the saying went, 'that's what friends are for.'

"Do you fancy him then?" Pamela said. She came part way up the stairs, so that her head was just above floor level. From there she saw Annabella observing Rutger.

"We're friends," Annabella said.

"I think you fancy him."

"I don't."

"Handsome enough to be in films," Pamela said, "and that South African accent makes me go all wobbly, don't it? So bloody manly it is. But a strange one is Rutger. Don't you think?"

"What's so strange about him?" Annabella asked.

"Friendly but not friendly. Not exactly a cold fish, mind you, but hardly warm. If you follow."

"He's a hard worker, and he likes it here," Annabella said, mostly from loyalty, since Pamela repeated every conversation to Gerald. "It's hard when you've grown up in two places, trying to figure out who you are. They made him study his course in Afrikaans until he was seven."

"What's that?"

"Nothing. He likes it here, Pamela ... you can trust me on that.

"That's nice then. Gerald said to tell you those reversible jacket things want taking back into the storeroom. They're not meant to be on the sale after all. Mr. Biddulph just called over from the Arndale."

Annabella kept silent.

"All right, then?"

"Yes. I'll tell Rutger."

"Thanks, Annabella."

Pamela banged her high heels down the stairs, safe again in Gerald's world.

Annabella crossed the floor to where Rutger had just finished labeling the jackets. "Gerald said, through Pamela mind you, that David Biddulph called over from the Arndale to say those jackets go back into the storeroom. They're not meant to be on sale."

"What?"

"That's what Pamela said."

Rutger's diffuse appearance changed. He drew back into himself and real anger simmered behind his eyes. For a moment she felt afraid. His hand clenched over the wire support of the clothes rack, then he closed his eyes, she imagined she saw his heart beat furiously under his shirt, an illusion of movement occurred there, as if the fabric actually rustled. She waited. His eyes didn't open, his fist didn't unclench. Again she felt afraid.

"Rutger?"

He said nothing.

"Rutger, what was it?"

He opened his eyes and looked at her and the fire quenched, the rage dissipated.

"Do you want me to put the jackets away?" she asked.

"Don't be daft," he said. "I'll bloody well do it."

He took them off the hangers, folded them into the box from which he took them half an hour before. A woman came in and looked at men's shoes, but she didn't speak. Annabella watched Rutger work, robot-like, his hands moving methodically. Where had he gone now, she wondered? This Rutger was neither scattered nor diffuse, the image of the mirror was no longer accurate; he was simply lost. How could she help him?

When he'd folded the last jacket she went up to him. "When's your next squash game?"

"I don't play anymore."

"Since when? You played with Gerald last week."

"No I didn't," he said. "It's a month ago at least."

"So why don't you play squash, then?"

"I run now."

"What do you mean run?"

"Jog." He moved his arms. "Run?"

"Oh," she said.

"For a while I swam at the pool in Heaton Park. But I gave it up because it was always too crowded. All of these arrogant school leavers and mums with kids. Now I run. It's nice ... I think ... I can feel like I'm flying ... like I'm, what? Escaping."

She thought about that a moment. "You run, Rutger, because there's something in you needs burned off."

For a knife-sharp moment he said nothing.

Then he said, in his harshly masculine Afrikaans tones, "Yes."

"And I don't know if running will do it."

He closed his eyes and this time she didn't mistake what she saw. His lower lip trembled. He opened his eyes and they looked squarely at one another. "No," he said.

Her heart ached. No other expression, she thought, described what she felt. She wanted to enfold him in her arms and cradle him. His sorrow filled her. She thought her own lower lip trembled. They continued to look at one another.

"That's the jackets then," Pamela announced from the top of the stairs.

Annabella turned and her cheeks scorched with a blush.

"That's the jackets then," Rutger said.

"Gerald will be pleased."

Rutger turned his head and Annabella clearly heard him whisper, "Bugger Gerald."

"That's good," Annabella said, fairly certain Pamela didn't hear Rutger's remark.

Pamela hung a moment at the top of the stairs, then she smiled and scurried down to the woman's department. When Annabella turned back Rutger had gone, only a movement of the curtain by the dressing rooms told her he'd taken the box of jackets into the storeroom. She reached into her pocket, took out his card, and read it one more time.

"There's no footpath here at all," Annabella said, "It's just a public golf course. We're going to be hit on the head by a ball."

The wind blew her hair like billowing sails.

"Are we heck." Rutger pointed to the appropriate page in the Manchester A-Z. "Look, it's a footpath."

"That squiggly line?"

"No. That's the power line, isn't it? Look," he said. "There. Follow my finger. See?"

"I don't know how you can tell a thing from that, really I don't. I'm sure we're where we're not meant to be and we're going to be run off by the police. I don't trust anything south of Withington."

"Don't be ignorant," he said. "It's a public footpath."

"Which is invisible to the human eye?"

He laughed. "I can't help it if the bastards let it grow over, can I?"

"I'm getting muddy," she shrieked. "Stripy bits all up the back of my trousers. They're just washed, these trousers."

"Annabella, do you want to hike with me or not?"

"I want to spend the day with you. That's the agreement. We're both off. No Gerald, no Pamela, no clothes ... to sell, I mean. When I rang you last night I was feeling sentimental, wasn't I? I thought how lovely it would be, two best friends, spending time together on their day off. This," she gestured, "well, this is maniacal then."

"This is good fun."

"Dodging golf balls?"

"We've not seen a single golf ball, have we?"

"You don't see them," she said. "They come flying at you at 100 kilometers per hour and strike you dead. Bang. No more Annabella."

"There's the spire. See."

She looked and saw a church spire rising above the trees at the edge of the golf course.

"You'll be glad," he said. "It's worth seeing." He brushed his hair back and when he scanned the horizon his eyes squinted slightly. She thought he looked particularly masculine today, in his dark blue wind cheater and worn jeans. Hard to mind a day spent in the company of a man as handsome as Rutger.

"But I want to talk to you," she said.

43

"What about?"

"Things we can't talk about at work."

He looked at her suspiciously.

"I'm not in love with you," she said. "It's not *that*."

"What then?"

"It's something else."

"What's 'something else' mean then, Annabella?"

"I have some opinions and I want to share them," she said.

"Opinions about what?"

"About you. About why you're so unhappy."

He looked straight at her. "That's you saying I'm unhappy again."

"That's me reaching out to you because I'm your friend. Can you understand that?"

He shrugged, a kind of rugged made-for-films shrug; he had presence her friend, Annabella thought, watching him; it was that rare thing, a real man.

"And so can we? Find time to talk, Rutger?"

He consulted the A-Z again, then he closed it and tucked it into the front pocket of his wind cheater. She saw that he hadn't shaved, dark brown beard shadow grizzled his chin, and perhaps the most handsome man she'd ever known. "And to think ..."

"What?" he said.

"What what?" she said.

"You said something."

"I didn't."

"You said 'and to think.'"

"I didn't."

"Annabella," he said patiently. "You did."

She looked stricken. "I'm thinking out loud, I am. That's what this hike of yours had done to me. I've gone round the bend."

He gently caressed her cheek. "Yes."

"*I have?*"

"I mean yes," he plunged forward across the golf course, "we'll find time to talk."

Rutger studied the eroded visage on the tomb, which looked as if the nose had been dissolved with acid. He heard Annabella's footsteps behind him. "There's some rugby-playing priest over here," he said. "He took one right on the nose, all right." Annabella offered no answer. "Come look." But when he turned he saw an unknown man. "Oh, sorry, I thought you were someone else."

"It's all right," Julian said, "I wish I were someone else."

They regarded one another a moment, then they smiled. The skinny man with an American accent wore a blue-striped shirt over a white 'T' shirt, accentuating his fragility. His cheekbones stood out with haunting emphasis, Rutger found it both a pretty and a frightening face, like the starving survivor of a concentration camp.

"American?" Rutger asked.

"They didn't give me a choice," Julian said.

"They don't, do they?"

"Never. I'd have gone for something glamorous if they did, Swedish perhaps."

They both laughed.

Kirsten came up beside them. "Hi," she said.

Neither of the men answered, Rutger unsure whether she spoke to him, Julian aware she didn't speak to him.

Annabella appeared from the crypt. "It's the world's best collection of mildew, that is. Reminds me of my French teacher at school. Mademoiselle Dumont. That's exactly what her jumpers smelt like, isn't it?" She noticed Kirsten and Julian. "Oh ..."

"Americans," Rutger said.

Annabella smiled, Kirsten smiled back, and no one said anything. Then Rutger and Annabella left. When they were outside the church Annabella hit him affectionately, and motioned to a bench beneath an oak tree. "Sit?"

"Why?"

She arched her brows.

"Oh. Right," he said. "I promised."

They sat down. A bird whistled plaintively on the church eaves. They watched it for several minutes.

"Well?" Rutger said.

She looked perturbed, holding her hair back from her face and peering at him.

"Just say what's on your mind then, Annabella."

"I think you're gay, Rutger."

He flushed. Quiet long moments filled up with bird song; neither spoke, nor did they look at each other.

Annabella finally broke the opaque silence, saying, "I don't think it's terrible or anything, I think it's fine, I do. But that's what I think's troubling you, that's why I think you're unhappy."

He still said nothing.   He looked away, noticing the rivers of moss on the bricks, how an oak tree filled up the space between the sacristy and the sky. What could he say to this? 'You've hit the nail on the head there, Annabella, my love.' 'I fancy men all right, Annabella, good on.'   His emotions quivered. Torn equally between confession and rejection, he wished himself far away, another planet perhaps. He wished himself to the very ends of the earth, where water thundered in cataracts off the edge of the known world and sea serpents played and no one could find him or know him or reach out to him. He desired oblivion and life at the same time. But this was Annabella sitting next to him, his friend, rejection was no easier than confession. Wishing himself far away was an impossibility, so he let the creeping paralysis hold him. He gave voice to no thoughts.

"*Rutger?*"

He resolutely refused to look at her, focusing instead on some hazy insinuation of Manchester skyline.

"But what do you think of what I said?"

He stood up. What did he think? Perhaps he thought nothing at all. "I think nothing at all," he said. "It's your opinion, not mine. I'm not required to think anything of your opinions am I?" He opened up his A-Z and consulted it.

She took his arm. "Don't shut me out, Rutger."

"You sound like bloody *Coronation Street*," he said.

"I want to talk."

"There's nothing to talk about." He looked at her then, and his eyes were beautifully soft and moist, not the usual eyes of Rutger van der Merwe. "I need to be getting back, don't I? I promised to put up some shelves for Mrs. Bennett. She's my mum's friend."

"You didn't mention those shelves before."

"I need to get back. That's that," he said. Then, "what makes you think I'm 'funny?'"

47

"I never said funny."

"Do I act a certain way?"

"There is no certain way that I know of."

"Is it the way I talk?" he asked.

"No, of course not."

"What, then?"

"It's intuition," she said, "It's just something I puzzled out." She let go of his arm. "Do you disagree with me?"

"I told you, I don't think anything about it, I don't disagree or agree."

"Are you or aren't you?"

"I think you've already decided."

"I expressed my opinion and there's nothing wrong with being gay," she said, "nothing at all."

"Did I say there was?"

"So do something about it," she said. "You're wasting your life."

"It's my life to waste, in case you hadn't noticed." He looked at his watch. "I need to catch the bus."

"There are more buses every hour of every day on the Wilmslow and Oxford Roads than any other roads in England. I read that somewhere. The one thing you do not need to do, Rutger, is catch a bus."

He sat back down again on the bench. Julian and Kirsten came out of the church. Rutger and Annabella kept silent. Kirsten waved at them and Rutger waved back. They waited until Julian and Kirsten disappeared into the graveyard, then Rutger took Annabella's face between his hands. "You're just about the best friend I've ever had. You know that. I think the world of you, but I'm not going to sit here on a bench in bleeding Didsbury and talk about whether or not I fancy shoving my prick up some good looking bloke's arse. Do you understand that?"

He released her face.

"Yes," she said.

"That's good then. Come on. I'll buy you an ice cream. You like ice creams."

She was silent.

"I know you heard me, Annabella."

She looked at him and there were tears in her eyes. "You're talking to me like a child now."

"I'm just making myself clear. Do you want an ice cream?"

"Yes," she said.

He stood up and offered her his hand. "Then let's go get you one. If you love me so much, you can't begrudge me an ice cream, can you?"

She said nothing. Bird song again filled the churchyard, an ambulance roared noisily down the Wilmslow Road toward the Manchester Royal Infirmary. "You're trying charm now to get rid of me, and it's not right, you're patronizing me. I mean well, you know I mean well."

"I know you do, Ronnie. I know you do."

She stood up. "All right, then. I can't begrudge you an ice cream, because I *do* love you."

Rutger jogged shirtless through Heaton Park, the long part of his fashionably cut hair, which he kept short on the sides, flopping down over his forehead. People looked at him, women looked at him, this slim-waisted, broad-shouldered young man with a model's face and an athlete's body. He noticed a pair of teenage girls positively make an exhibition over him near the tea stand. And why shouldn't they? Wasn't that why he wore left his shirt behind? So that he'd be ogled? Or did it have an even deeper significance today, something to do with Annabella and their conversation in Didsbury? The Rutger van der Merwe who chose the manly sport of rugby as his life's passion didn't want to think about that conversation, because he didn't want to consider what it meant, didn't want to reflect on whether Annabella was right or wrong. He didn't want to turn a corner in life, admit something about his sexual desire, and find himself suddenly a thing with a label like 'crippled Mr. Haggerty,' 'blind Mrs. Thompson,' 'old Sam,' 'that ugly Shoemaker daughter' ... 'that poofter son of Mrs. Whitaker's' ... or someone talked about smarmily in Parliament, 'the rights of ho-mo-sex-uals.'

Rutger wanted only to savor the breeze touching the sweat beneath his chest hair, the appreciative glances of passersby, the birds singing in the thick trees by the lake, the wonderful exhilaration of his calf muscles and the blood as it pulsed in his thighs. The majority of people didn't like what gay men did to each other, he thought, and if the wiring in your circuits inclined you to do those things, like slipping your willy up the poop chute, or taking it in your gob ... well, where did that leave you? It might sicken the neighbors to think of a man who could be a recruiting poster for Her Majesty's forces fucking the lights out of their son, but what if nothing else even began to feel normal to you? What did you do? Things which felt abnormal to you? Nothing? Deny yourself? Find some woman to torment with your inadequacy? Normal was a feeling as well as a convention, Rutger thought, and when the feeling conflicted with the convention ... you had a big problem.

He came out of the park on Sheepfoot Lane and darted across the traffic on the Bury Old Road. An ugly poster which read

STOP THE DESTRUCTION OF WHITEFIELD:

HALT CONSTRUCTION OF THE M62 TRUNK

, which represented the politically correct opinion for Prestwich, and not only Rutger's but everyone he knew, had been defaced with paint which, although utterly incorrect politically said, as if it were poetry,

Ever sit
In the queue
On the M62?

He ran back through the Sainsbury's carpark and the drab shopping precinct surrounding it. The salesman in Dixon's noticed him, people in cars parked against bollards in the carpark noticed him, people loading groceries noticed him, a delivery man offloading kegs of beer at the pub noticed him, an assortment of people in Northern England in the waning hours of a workday all noticed him. Rutger stopped at the Pelican light on the Bury New Road, and having stopped the air felt cool against his skin.

"Hello, Rutger," Mrs. Bennet said, her arms loaded with bags.

"Hello," he said, then touching his flat stomach, "running," by way of excusing himself from carrying her groceries. Once trapped in Mrs. Bennet's kitchen you didn't escape quickly. What if she knew he fancied diddling her grandson Edgar, the gorgeous blond one at university in Leicester? That would stop the cream cakes in their tracks.

"Oh," she said, "you'll catch your death."

"Will I heck, it's a warm day today."

"Strange summer all around I say."

"Is it?"

"Oh yes, why ..."

The light changed and the signal warbled. With an apologetic wave he dashed over the tarmac and down the leafy lane by the church, then up through the graveyard. The Sebastopol headstone, as the neighborhood called it, blocked his path and, as usual, he veered around it. He'd been only twenty-three years old, this officer who died for Queen and country in the far-off Crimea, and whose remains they carted across the Mediterranean and back ... somehow, inexplicably really ... to Prestwich. Rutger had an image for a moment of the man's skeleton, and then of the man himself, perhaps with shining black hair full of pomade, a roguish eye, perhaps out for some Saturday night fun in his uniform, polished belt buckle, scrubbed shoe leather.

The Vicar appeared suddenly at the doorway to the church, grey-muzzled Labrador at his side, forcing Rutger almost to collide with him.

"Evening," Rutger said, slowing.

"*Oh, my,*" came the gasp, startled perhaps, or impressed by the sight of this muscled hairy chest jogging through his churchyard, "Oh yes, good evening, then."

The dog barked.

Rutger waved over his shoulder ... none of his family were churchgoers, and the Vicar's local standing didn't demand excessive courtesy these days ... as he pushed down the hill, out the iron gate, up the next street and then through the alley to the street where he spent his youth. When back at the house he ran upstairs to shower, and then stood for a moment at the window, staring into the neighbor's back garden. The family's three year old twins played there amongst a riot of lobelia and pansies, a pretty picture, England as the Tory's imagined England. He heard the twins' young voices, squabbling over who got to push their pretend vacuum cleaner, one threatened to tell mum on the other. Then turning back to the bathroom Rutger noticed that his mother had cleaned it that morning, it glistened with the house proud antiseptic air he associated with her. Even the spigots gleamed.

He'd never been so depressed, he thought suddenly, and losing his balance he nearly brought down the shower curtain. He didn't want to work in a clothing store, he wanted to do something else with his life. He wanted to be a teacher, like his father.

And he wanted to accept being gay.

In the implosion of silence which seemed to follow his realizations he heard the far-off clatter of a Metrolink train, and then he remembered his conversation with Annabella and his eyes smarted. Then, as he dropped his shorts, he saw himself in the mirror, lean and muscled, handsome, athletic, and touching himself he grew hard.

Brooke sat at a sea-front table at Back on the Beach Cafe, off Pacific Coast Highway in Santa Monica, waiting to meet Wyatt for lunch. A breeze frisked her hair. Across from her, in the shade, sat a television celebrity. Although Brooke glanced in that direction now and again, she refused to look directly. Homage to a media personality seemed ... well, unsure just what it seemed, she knew she wouldn't do it. Two muscled young men practiced volleyball serves at the public nets. Brooke watched their athletic grace, their effortless strength like the artwork of testosterone. Such handsome young men, it resembled a cinematic image, the sort of thing a woman looked for at the beach on a mid-80's, bright blue, summer breezy Southern California day. Years ago that would have been Wyatt. She remembered how Wyatt regularly attended the beach, tan as a walnut, a tousle-haired hunk. Again she observed the volleyball boys. As they bounced the ball back and forth, they talked about something which made them laugh, but Brooke couldn't hear what. Looking at their tensed masculine cords of abdominal muscle she thought: those boys haven't given birth, and then, of course, she reflected on how she gave birth to George.

Brooke frowned upon her self-awareness. Weren't the insane the most introspective of all, Ophelia and Lear and various drooling Faulkner characters? Self-aware people were too subjective, they spun tales, they saw things, they heard voices. Brooke had long known that when too self-aware she manipulated things, making external reality conform to the shifting sands of her moods. Her moods shifted plenty of sand too, in fact she'd back-hoed a couple of dunes recently. Yesterday, in the kitchen, running the blender, she heard George's voice -- it came from the direction of the empty apple juice bottle on the sideboard. Worst of all, self-aware people, finely tuned to their inner universe, bored others. How many times had she mocked Julian for his ability to bore people? Brooke didn't want to be like that. Just as she tried to think about something other than herself and her feelings, Wyatt came along the boardwalk, paused to take off his shoes and then trudged to her table ... which, of course, she'd chosen because it was farthest away. The tables at Back on the Beach Cafe nestled in the sand, and nearly everyone took his shoes off. Wyatt kissed her cheek and sat down with a heavy sigh.

Wyatt looked like someone who'd been on a bender, hollow-cheeked, sallow, an unpleasant contrast to the muscled young men practicing volleyball. Brooke looked away from him. She stared a long while at the breakers, and then at a health club about two miles away, at the intersection of Sunset and Pacific Coast Highway. It had attractive concrete architecture.

"What are you thinking about?" Wyatt asked.

"Nothing ... politics."

"What about politics?" he wondered.

"I don't know," she said.

"You're thinking about something but you don't know what you're thinking about it?"

Wyatt had an engineer's mind. 'Odious little man,' Brooke thought, as if he were Tansley in *To the Lighthouse*, her -- and Julian's, unfortunately -- favorite novel. Virginia Woolf would have found Wyatt illustrative of linear sequentiality, Brooke thought, and then she decided that Virginia Woolf was too self-aware if anyone was.

"Does it matter what I'm thinking?" she challenged.

"Usually," Wyatt said.

She thought about that, then she lowered her sunglasses and peered at him over the top of them as she said. "God exists in the pectorals of those beautiful young men ... if he exists at all."

This took the wind completely out of Wyatt's sails. He merely stared at her, with a cursory glance toward the volleyball nets.

"Do you think he exists?" Brooke asked.

"God? I ... well, not in somebody's chest muscles, but ... more or less, sure, I guess."

Brooke put her sunglasses on. "I used to have great tits."

He said quietly, "You still do."

"No, they're okay, but they're not great. I'm like a piggy that suckled her young ... which I did, suckle my young, I mean."

They were quiet.

"I can't follow this conversation," Wyatt said.

"It's not a conversation, it's some kind of question and answer thing."

"Can   we   have   a   conversation?"
"I   imagine."

However, they were simply quiet for a long while. The waitress hovered, saw they weren't ready to order, and disappeared.

"Excuse me," Brooke suddenly shouted. She stood up and started moving toward the volleyball nets. "Excuse me."

"Huh?" the nearest young man asked.

Wyatt realized, in an uncharacteristic blossoming of intuition, that she prepared to consult with a third party about her breasts. In attempting to stand up too quickly, however, he sprawled over backwards in the sand. It forced Brooke to turn around and upside down he saw her face, a three-eyed slithery monster's face bearing down upon him.

"I'm sorry," he said, still lying in the sand.

The television celebrity watched them intently, having taken off her sunglasses to see better.

"Tell me about it," Brooke snapped, giving Wyatt a hand.

"Alec," Kirsten said, "it was terrible."

"Where's he now?"

"In the shower. He's been in there for ages."

"Rehydrating. Those plane flights suck out your moisture like you're an apricot half in a fruit dryer."

"I'm still shaken up. It was a terrible scene, really terrible."

"Ah, lovey, I knew ... I really did ... and I'm sorry."

"Alec, he ... just acts normal ... Like he's here as a tourist," Kirsten told him. "It's agonizing."

"I'll come home," Alec said.

"Now?" Kirsten asked.

"Yes. I can be there in twenty minutes. We'll all talk."

" He'll think something's wrong."

"Something is wrong."

"But it's not good for him to think there is. Don't you agree?"

"All right," Hayley said. "But let's do something tomorrow, the three of us."

"I'm meant to work tomorrow."

"I thought you were taking two weeks holiday."

"Three weeks, but not starting until Monday. I'm meant to work all this week."

"That's not acceptable. Ring them this afternoon and arrange the rest of this week. Honestly, Kirsten, nothing short of that will keep you sane. Trust me. You know I'm right."

"Maybe. They know about George, and Julian's role and all of that. Yes, I'm sure they'd understand at work." It stayed quiet for a few crackling moments. Then Kirsten said, "I'm wondering if maybe you weren't right. That having Julian here is a mistake."

"Of course it's a mistake," Alec said, "but there's no turning back now. And who knows? Maybe you will be able to help him."

"I don't know."

Kirsten took a breath, and as she did she caught a reflection of herself in the mirror above the fireplace. Her hair disarranged, her face flushed, my God, she thought in horror, she'd become middle-aged, he'd done this to her, her own brother, he'd pushed her across the threshold into middle age. Her pulse accelerated. "Alec, I look hideous. In the mirror, just now. I look like Baba Yaga, warts, wrinkles, hairs sprouting from my chin, I've aged twenty years. Oh, God. I do. I look absolutely hideous. Disgusting. Like a middle-aged harridan."

"Stop this," Alec said.

"I can't."

"You must. Come to a place where you have perspective. Look, write this title down. Do you have a pen?"

"Yes."

"*Give Me Room.* Did you get that? By Muriel Whippet."

"Whip it?"

"Like the dog, dear. Really. That's the book for you, it's all based on Virginia Woolf. At least I think it's Virginia Woolf. At any rate," Hayley said, "it'll teach you how to find and keep perspective. The secretaries here claim that the tips on masturbating are out of this world, though you needn't pay attention to that part. Who knows? It's up to you. All right?"

"All   right   what?"

"All   right   in   general."

Kirsten heard Julian's footsteps overhead. She had to fix her hair and touch up her face, so she said, "Yes. I need to go now. Thanks for the chat. And thanks for tomorrow. I'll see you this evening. And thanks."

Brooke pulled up at the address in Mar Vista that the elementary school she, Kirsten and Julian attended in Santa Monica had given to her. The 50s-looking stucco building -- which more or less defined Mar Vista, Brooke thought uncharitably -- stretched back from droughted lawn. A vandalism-stunted magnolia tree leaned toward the walkway, crusty parking lot embraced a green-lettered sign, which dwarfed its surrounding bed of geraniums. Through the glass front door a man in a wheelchair looked on a brown-sky world. Brooke let herself out, locked, engaged the alarm, and went slowly up the path. The door pulled outward and a rush of cool medicinal air hit her. Hadn't she read that people judge nursing homes by their smell? The man in the wheelchair looked up at her expectantly. But it was only Brooke, no one important, not a son or daughter. He glanced away again, out toward the street.

The place absorbed her into its odorous hush.

Brooke moved forward on the yellowish linoleum. Beyond the lobby as many as thirty people sat in a lounge and stared. Several slept. One or two of them chatted. Banks of walkers formed a corral. Brooke stood by a plastic potted palm. No one seemed particularly to notice her, although several faces briefly looked in her direction. One man pointed a cane at her quizzically, let it drop, and ignored her. She looked around the room until she identified Mrs. Anderson. She sat alone in knee high nylon stockings and a beige house dress, her head thrown back in sleep, a white knitted sweater pulled around her shoulders. Her pale face crumpled with wrinkles, a rat's nest of white hair frizzed around her scalp.

Mrs. Anderson had been Brooke's Kindergarten teacher, someone from the time Brooke was George's age. She looked a long while at Mrs. Anderson. This felt like oblivion, forgotten time, nothingness, this summed up everything Brooke feared most. She willed herself to go up to her old teacher, to awaken her, to speak to her. After all, she'd gone to this much trouble. Mrs. Anderson dropped her jaw in a snore. In the end Brooke did go over, sat down beside her and took her hand. She woke up, looked Brooke directly in the face and smiled.

"Your hand's awfully warm," she said.

"Do you remember me?"

"Are you Helen? From next door? Down to Redondo Beach?"

"No. I was your student, in Santa Monica. Brooke Hathaway?"

Mrs. Anderson drew a blank. "An awful long time ago." She shook her head. "You're not here trying to sell me something, are you?"

"Of course not. I came to see you."

"How come?"

"Because you were important to me."

"What was your name again?"

"Brooke Hathaway, though my last name's Eiffel now, I'm married. I had a little boy named George, but he died, he drowned down at Corona del Mar ... because his uncle didn't watch him at the beach."

"Oh, Sweetie, I'm sorry."

"Thank you."

"Do you have any others?"

"No."

"Having some others is important, I saw that on Oprah. It was either Oprah or Ellen, I'm not sure which, but I think it was Oprah. I watch an awful lot of TV."

Brooke ignored Oprah's opinion on having replacement children. "If you don't remember me," she said, "then I don't suppose you remember the time I

asked you over for dinner and you said no."

"Dinner? At your parents' house?"

"You said no."

"I *never*."

"It's true," Brooke said.

"Why'd I say no?"

"You said that once you got home and took your girdle off you didn't go out again, except maybe to go to the grocery store."

"Lordy. I told you that?"

"Yes," Brooke said.

"Didn't even go out to the grocery store much, truth be told. But I can't for the life of me imagine turning down a chance to go eat. No ma'am. What on earth was possessing me?"

"I always respected the fact that you wouldn't come."

"Why?"

"Thumbing your nose at pretense."

"Was your family pretentious?"

"Well, no, that's not really what I mean. Ignoring the pressure, you know, that kind of thing."

"Why would I want to go and do that?" She shook her head. "You aren't making much sense, my dear."

"I guess not," Brooke said.

Mrs. Anderson looked long at her. "You had a sister."

"Yes. Kirsten."

"Kirsten Hathaway. What a pretty little girl. That was your sister?"

"Still is."

"I might just remember you then. Real competitive kid."

"That was me."

Mrs. Anderson smiled. "Oh my, yes, yes I do remember. But I sure as heck don't remember turning you down for dinner. You sure you aren't making that part up?"

"I'm sure."

"It's very sweet of you to come all the way out here to see me," Mrs. Anderson said, in a faint reminder of her teacher-polite voice. "I don't think there's any point in having dinner with your family now."

"No."

"You still think of me? From those long ago days?"

"They aren't so long ago really."

"Maybe not. Sure does warm a teacher's heart."

"You taught me something special," Brooke said.

"I'm glad then. Real glad."

Brooke looked at her watch, leaned forward, and kissed Mrs. Anderson's cheek. "Take care, Mrs. Anderson."

"You too ... I'm sorry, I've gone and forgotten your name again."

"Brooke. Brooke Eiffel."

"Oh, land's sake. Of course. Well, you too, Brooke. You take care too. And I'm real sorry about your youngster. That's a terrible thing. And not to make light of a tragedy, but you and your husband have you some more, that's the ticket."

"Of course," Brooke said. "That's the ticket."

4

Kirsten heard Julian on the staircase. Her body tensed, she felt as if her back arched, her hair stood on end. For a moment her thoughts flew helter-skelter. She even lost her own name. Who was she? Then everything rushed back in at her. What could it mean when your brother affected you this way?

"Nice shower?" she asked.

"Hot."

"Isn't that what makes a shower nice?"

"Yes," he said, "I suppose so. Is something bothering you, Kirsten? I know your tones of voice and that tense face you're making. It's me, isn't it?" he   asked.

She could say nothing, her lips would not have formed words if she tried.

"It's   all   right,   Kirsten."

She found her words at last. "Thanks. But honestly, I don't want to talk about my feelings right now."

He lifted up his palms and said, "Hey, no prob." He sat on the sofa opposite her. They stared at one another.

"Alec's taking us someplace tomorrow. I'm going to ask for more time off work. Is there any place you'd especially like to see?"

"I don't know." He thought a moment. "Blackpool maybe."

"*Blackpool?*"

"Sure. Why not? It's summer, it's a seaside resort."

"Okay," she said. "Blackpool." Kirsten felt herself grow tense again. "Want to go for a walk?"

she asked. "Shake your muscles loose? I always like to walk after I've been cooped up in an airplane."

"Okay," he said.

She found the keys on the bookcase in the hall and led them out to the street. They went to the bottom of the cul-de-sac, through the pathway and out to the shops, where Didsbury Village straggled along both sides of the Wilmslow Road, with trendy upscale green grocers, *Est, Est, Est* Italian restaurant, a petrol station, a cutesy Londonesque cheese store with Blue Stiltons in painted pots. "It's an embarrassment, that cheese store," Alec always said, though Kirsten did not understand why. She thought it sweet, the store clerks wore checked skirts and little green aprons. The blustery wind pulled against her hair. She thought of saying something about it, but when she turned to Julian she noticed his preoccupation, his face drawn up in a self-absorbed scowl, and so she said nothing. Quiet felt better anyway. They walked toward the gardens behind the church. If the sun did come out, it would be warmest there.

Although the middle of a work day, a surprising number of people were about. A bus hurtled by. In the wake of its fumy cacophony Kirsten and Julian walked in silence. Without noticing the wild roses, which Kirsten had meant to point out to him, Julian went sullenly through the gate before her. She hung back, watching his ugly clomp-clomp on the gravel. In the sunlight his pallor and his wretched thinness were shocking, even with a thick cotton shirt and a 'T' shirt underneath she saw his ribs. The back of his head, the way he held his hands, they reminded her uncomfortably of a prisoner.

She didn't want Julian to remind her of a prisoner.

"Let's sit," she said. "Those benches are sheltered. It won't be windy there."

They sat side-by-side.

"Do you think this blouse suits me?" she asked.

"It's pretty." Then, "When you ask me questions like that," he said, "it's like we're still in high school. I can see you at the top of the stairs, yelling down at me, 'but does it make my eyes look cute?'"

"And you said, 'no matter what you wear they'll still be crossed.'"

"And you freaked," he said, "because then you thought they really must be crossed."

"How geekish."

"No, you were adorably gullible. It's one of your nicest traits, Kirsten. You believe in ... well, things ... things and people. It's who you are."

"Yes," she said, although she wasn't happy with that being who she was. "Do you ever see -- what was the guy's name? The one you lived with? David?"

"Hardly. He moved to Atlanta."

"Talk to him then. Whatever."

"I sent him a card, this great Britts photograph, sweaty mechanic heaving around iron implements. David's kind of card. He never answered. David doesn't do tragedy well, he's probably afraid I'll expect him to come back to me as a sympathy case or something. I could have predicted he'd ignore me."

"I'm sorry,' Kirsten said. "I don't know how you stop loving someone." She couldn't imagine being told she must stop loving Alec. It would be impossible.

"I dwell on him sometimes," Julian said. "But, I like have other things to worry about now. You know?"

It fell quiet. Neither one spoke.

Then Kirsten said, "Remember that time we all went on a camping trip to Arizona? You and Brooke zipped me out of the tent when I went to the bathroom."

"Well, for God's sake, Kirsten, you went to the bathroom about ten times a night," he said. "You had the worst bladder control in history."

"I think I had a bladder infection, actually. Did you know I cut my nose trying to get back in?"

"Poor baby," he laughed.

"Yeah ... you two giggled in your sleeping bags the rest of the night. I always felt so excluded from the little world the two of you had."

"That's not something you'll need to worry about anymore then, is it?"

They fell silent once more and observed a toddler with her mother. The mother tore off a spray of Rose of Sharon blossoms and the child giggled as the flowers touched her face. For a few moments Kirsten thrilled to the sight, then suddenly she felt odd, a feeling like being a poor hostess. Did this trouble Julian? Watching a mother with her child? Shouldn't she do something?

"We don't need to sit here," she said. "I mean, if you'd rather walk."

He gestured out toward the child and mother. "I don't mind."

The mother and child continued to play together.

"We could look at the church," Kirsten said.

"Just there." She pointed. "It has a medieval tomb or a famous pulpit, I don't recall. Something historic."

"Sure," he said, "fine."

They rose together and walked along the gravel path toward the church. Without meaning to she brushed against him. He must have thought it intentional, because he smiled and took her hand and held it as they walked. Well, she thought, it felt nicer than fighting, and nicer than expressing her mind.

"Feeling better?" he asked.

"Than what?" she said.

He laughed out loud, but she caught the unmistakable coldness behind his barked laugh. Their eyes met and she shrugged.

"We'll get through this," he said.

She glanced at him and saw that his eyes had a shadowy cast, smudges beneath shadows. She looked away. "I'm doing just fine, you know, Julian ... so, I'm not sure what you mean by the 'we'll' part of that."

He turned to her in surprise, seemed to understand the sense of her remark and said, "If it looks like I'm not going to get through this thing then I'll go home. Promise." He tried to make her look him in the face. She felt his hot scrutiny. "A deal, Kirsten?"

She bucked up her courage and looked at him again, but all she could do was shrug, as her eyes filled large with tears.

Brooke stood in the center of Julian's living room. Tattered Persian rugs, homey furniture, polo prints on the walls, dull brass sconces with candles at the ready for power failures, books everywhere, unpolished wooden floors, orchestrated English, stage-settish, a mock-up of a Berkshire country cottage. Did he use a magazine photograph as a guide, or did it come to him through intuition?

As she ran a hand along the back of the sofa, snagging at threads with her nails, slitting open the seam of a pillow, she prayed that England would be a let down to Julian. She hoped it wouldn't measure up to his need for it. Here, alone with Julian's possessions, she easily imagined his sleepless nights, his despondence. Suffering oozed from the walls. This pleased her. She wondered how her brother, who so carefully polished his furniture and so painstakingly arranged his books, could so carelessly murder her baby?

She walked into Julian's bedroom.

She sat down at Julian's desk, which remained just as Julian left. The fact unnerved her. It felt wrong. So she tipped all of the drawers out on the floor and, for good measure, jabbed at papers with her foot, crinkled their edges, crumpled his envelopes. That felt better. She ran her diamond ring over the burnished desk top, only stopping when she came to the framed row of photographs which faced her. From her seat she saw out the window, across the alley, into the parking lot of a discount drug store chain. An ugly view, it made her smile with pleasure. She wouldn't have wanted Julian's suffering to be alleviated by a pretty view.

She'd never been in Julian's bedroom before. She prized open his filing cabinet with an old metal ruler she found lying amid the wreckage on the floor. The top drawer contained a manuscript, which Brooke was not inclined to read, and several ski-resort brochures. She opened the window and tossed the manuscript out into the alley. Papers fluttered over the fence. Some fell into the apartment's swimming pool. She liked that, she thought they'd probably clog the filter. The bottom drawer held some graded and ungraded papers, while the center drawer held pens, pencils, erasers, and bottles of liquid paper. She scooped everything up in her hands and threw it across the floor, like sprinkling rose petals at a wedding. A stubborn bottle of liquid paper she hurled through the door into the hallway.

One of the framed photographs on the desk held Brooke's attention, Julian on a camping trip, probably in Europe, since the Peugeot which could just be glimpsed in the background appeared to have a French license plate. At least five years ago, Julian looked in peak condition, long before he developed into a scarecrow. She didn't like seeing him fit, she preferred him as a droopy-clothed AIDS wannabe. In the photograph, he shaved at a small oval mirror nailed to a tree, dressed only in a pair of olive pants with a brown belt. A pinkish towel hung round his neck, his jaw smeared with shaving foam and his hair wet; he seemed rapt in concentration.

Behind him she saw a yellow and red tent. What made the photograph so provocative was that amid the squalor of a camping trip Julian looked like a model, invigorated and handsome. This might be how someone on Madison Avenue posed him, how an advertiser sold camping in the Auvergne. Brooke wondered what Julian saw in the mirror that day. The face of a future murderer? Julian's sense of detachment was what Brooke used to admire most in him. That such a man should murder her son had become the enigma within the mystery. Brooke picked the photograph up and brought it close to her face, close enough to see that the Peugeot's license plate was French after all. Then she threw the photograph out the window too.

She heard it splash into the swimming pool.

Another photograph was of Kirsten, in a string bikini, on a beach which Brooke guessed to be in Hawaii. She looked vulnerable, the way Kirsten often did, peering at the camera as if it threatened. In the water, about to dive into a wave, Brooke made out a man, whose back she recognized as Julian's. Who took this photograph? Brooke scanned it, saw it all as the photographer must have.

Kirsten's innocence has been magically captured on film. And even the disappearing Julian seemed portentous. Would the photograph have meant the same thing if Kirsten and Julian were standing arm-in-arm? For an instant Brooke suffered a deep pang, it felt as if Kirsten were the one who was dead; as if Kirsten were the one she might never see again. In that moment Brooke knew just how much she loved her sister. She also realized that she was the photographer who captured this on film. This photograph she cradled lovingly, replacing it where it had been on the desk top. This one wouldn't go in the pool.

She hunted₁ through the house from top to bottom, destroying as she went. Beyond the apartment's extreme tidiness, which made it a delight to wreak havoc, she marveled at the organization -- stackable closet units, precise folded piles of trousers, color-ordered shirts, alphabetized books. She soon remedied all this, however, by her heaving, tossing and dumping. When the thought came to her, she immediately went down on her hands and knees beneath the desk and carved grooves with her key on the floor. She rolled up Julian's little antique carpet, which he bought or\ne summer in Paris, put it in the bathtub and turned the shower on it. She knew the wool would be ruined. She could see where it had been taped to the floor, a faint change detectable in the color of the wood.

The desk and chair she moved, so that they blocked the closet. There were thin scrapes left behind from one of the desk legs. Brooke felt pleased by her activity. When finally she came to the end of destroying and saw she had made an absolute tip of the place, she sat on the window seat and considered the view of the drugstore parking lot.

She felt pleased with her day's work.

Saturday night crowds packed the restaurant, but from their advertised scenic window they saw nothing of suburban Alderly Edge but blurry trees and a carpark. They drank their locally brewed lagers, while Julian merely nibbled at his meal and Kirsten and Alec ate theirs. Although Alec ordered them chocolate torte, they merely prodded it without enthusiasm, polite in the way of strangers. When they finished and settled the bill, they walked along the drizzly streets, windows easier to peer into than each other's minds. For a moment, as they crossed the street to an art gallery, Kirsten successfully pretended they were happy. She saw them as observers might see them, upwardly mobile Saturday night people, a pleasant image. But the reflection of the three of them in the gallery's bay window brought the unpleasant truth home.

"We don't have to see the film ... if you don't want to," Kirsten said.

"I don't mind." Julian said.

They stayed quiet for a long while. Alec had met someone he knew and was engaged in a conversation about a student who died of alcohol poisoning the night before. Kirsten and Julian stood several feet from him, limp and ungiving.

"Julian?" Kirsten asked.

"What?"

"You've been quiet for so long."

"I'm sorry," he said softly.

"No, no, don't apologize ... I didn't mean it that way."

"What's the film again?"

"French? I can't remember the name. Alec says it's funny."

He turned fully to her. "I shouldn't have come over here, Kirsten. You can't make things be what they're not. I was wrong, very wrong." He sighed and turned away.

Although she did not feel close to him -- perhaps she even felt repelled by him -- she nonetheless wanted to do something for him. That was her nature. But she couldn't think what to say, so she continued to stand limply.

"I envy you," he said. "All of this," he waved, "Alec, England, all of it." He turned back to her. "What a hell of a mess I've made of my life, Kirsten ... what a hell of a mess."

Annabella watched NRJ Hits with her sister. Sprawling over the sofa, bathed and with her hair freshly washed, she felt sleepy. Her feet touched against the bookcase on the far wall. Though she got in trouble once for putting her feet on it, now no one seemed to care. She cried when she was ten and her dad told her 'take your feet off the bleeding bookcase.' It was the way he told her, of course, as if she mattered less than the wall, because even at the age of ten she understood the logic of not banging holes in the wall. She looked over at her sister, then she took her feet off the bookcase.

"Oh, it's a real bore this is," her sister said.

"It isn't," Annabella said. "I like it."

"They're pulling it off the tube, aren't they? It's a bore."

"It's been given a reprieve."

"It doesn't bloody do anything."

"It's not supposed to do anything," Annabella told her. "It shows you the charts, lets you see what singers look like. It's light entertainment."

Her sister wrinkled her nose. "Don't you have any plans for tonight then?"

"No."

"God, look at that stupid bitch," her sister said, with reference to a singer in a black mini-skirt and gold bra. "It's like she's trying to suck off the microphone, isn't it? Oh, that's disgusting. How can you watch this rubbish?"

"It's no worse than MTV."

"Well?" Her sister asked importantly. "Have you seen me watching MTV?"

The doorbell went. Neither one of them moved.

"I can't go," Annabella said. "Look at me."

"You're lazy you are, Annabella. *Lazy.*"

"It's my day off."

"It's not 'day' anymore. It's night."

"It's the night of my day off then."

Her sister got up with a groan and went into the hall.   A moment later Rutger preceded her through the door.

"Rutger," Annabella said, leaping from the sofa. "I just had a bath. I'm all soggy."

"You look fine, Annabella. I was wondering if we could talk."

Her sister watched Rutger from the doorway. She raised her eyebrows and fanned herself. 'You're the stupid bitch,' Annabella thought, 'he doesn't fancy your flabby bum, that's for sure.'

"Here   you   mean?"   Annabella   asked.

"It doesn't matter where. Let's go for a drink. Can   we   walk   somewhere?"

She looked at the clock. "Sure, yeah." NRJ Hits embarrassed her, and she clicked the television off.   "If   you   don't   care   how   I   look."

"I think you look fine."

"Suits me, then," she shrugged.   "Are you paying?"

"Yes."

5

They went into the hall and toward the door, Annabella's sister following behind making even more obnoxious moues. Clearly she never expected a man this desirable to call for Annabella. Rutger and Annabella went outside, the door slammed behind them.

"Pretty girl, your sister." Rutger said.

"Don't let her hear you say it. She fancies you."

"I'll bite my tongue."

"She'd rather bite it for you," Annabella said. "This way."

She led him through the park. A faint breeze rustled the oaks, a man played Frisbee with his dog, an elderly couple sat on a bench bundled up in cardigans. In the dry basin of the old fountain a cigarette pack blew in a circle. The metal-on-metal wail of a train on the metrolink line broke the stillness. It faded away. Neither Rutger nor Annabella spoke, as they crossed the width of the park and went into the nearly-empty pub. A popular dance song played on the jukebox. Rutger got the drinks and brought them back to the table where Annabella sat.

She sipped her beer. "What's on your mind then, Rutger?"

"I didn't treat you properly yesterday."

"I know that."

"So first off, I want to apologize. Secondly, I want to share my thoughts with you. If you'll listen."

She looked at him. Something had happened to him, she thought, he looked lighter, he seemed freer. "What's caused this change of heart?"

"I thought about what you said." He drank a long gulp of his bitter and across his face played strong emotions. "Thing is, Annabella, being ... gay is about more than sex, that's why it's so frightening like, it's a statement about your whole psychology, isn't it? It defines how you see the world. I suppose, for lack of a better word it's ... political."

His whispered, the dangerous word hanging over them.

"Political?"

"Yes."

"Are you telling me you agree with me, Rutger? About being gay?"

He peered at her from out of his beer and his eyes momentarily looked like an animal caught in car headlamps.

She touched his hand and he allowed it. "So why didn't you say so yesterday? And why come all this way to tell me now?"

"It's not such a long way."

"Don't be difficult."

"Because I owed you. Do you want to hear what I thought this afternoon?" he asked.

"All right then," she said, and she saw that it became less difficult for him.

"The thing is, I'm not looking for sex. I mean sex is not what it's all about. It's about intimacy. Almost anyone can find someone for sex."

"I don't know about my cousin Maria," Annabella said, "she doesn't shave properly like."

Rutger looked away a moment, as if her humor disconcerted him. He struggled to find his words again, and she regretted her crack. He thought of what to say, and continued, "If built only upon sex then a relationship is bound to be ... rotten. It has to be built off intimacy."

"What do you mean by intimacy, then?"

"You know, dead of night, quiet, unquantifiable things."

"Unquantifiable?"

"You know."

"But sex is tied into it," Annabella said, "sex expresses intimacy."

"So I can't avoid sex, and maybe I can't say I'm not looking for it." He paused and looked out the window, "Yes, I am looking for sex, of course I am. I'm being daft. But I don't think I'm looking very hard."

"You have to look when you're hard," she said.

"*Annabella*," he protested.

"Sorry. It's very self-aware, to think all that," she said and then she quietly twisted her hair.

"I think a lot about things, because I want to be sure my life is," he seemed to search for words, gave it up and shrugged, "You know. Consequential like."

"You're talking like you went to bleeding public school," she said.

"You know what consequential means, you're sending me up now."

"I'm not."

"Then don't be a snob," he said, "because you know I don't put airs on, so don't say it." They looked at one another a moment, and Annabella looked away first. "Something significant happened yesterday. Didn't it?"

"I think so," she said.

"I feel like a tuning fork which has been struck too hard, you know? Like the sound of that breaking string in The Cherry Orchard."

"That Russian play?"

"Yeah. That Russian play," he echoed. And he spoke truth. Vibrations from the conversation with Annabella continued to resonate. It felt the way things felt the night his father died. Half an hour before dad's heart attack they celebrated his birthday: streamers, cake, laughter, music. Then dad went upstairs, sat on the toilet, and died, slumped against the wall. Today felt as painfully extraordinary as that night. On one level it even felt exhilarating. Things happened, and having happened, they existed.

"Do you think the neighbor children are going to call me a poofter and paint things on our front wall?" he asked.

"I don't know," she said, "this is Prestwich not London. Are you afraid of yobbos painting things on your mum's wall?"

"I'll fucking bash their heads in."

"If you find them."

"I'll find them," he said.

"How will they know?" she asked.

"Because I don't intend to keep who I am a secret, you know me better than that."

She nodded in agreement. They looked at one another, then she looked away from him and he watched her draw a circle in the beer which had spilled on the table top. She still didn't look at him.

"One more thing," he said. "I'm going to go to uni ... and become a teacher."

"How's that to do with being gay?"

"I don't know really. But I'm going to do it."

"Can you?" she asked honestly, face to the table.

"Maybe," he said.

"You have to get into college first."

"I know it can be done," he said. Then he asked, "Do you know how This Side of Paradise ends?"

"Is it a book?"

80

"Brilliant book. American. 'He stretched out his arms to the crystalline, radiant sky. 'I know myself,' he cried, 'but that is all.'"

"This Side of Paradise is it?"

"I'm not sending you up, Annabella, and I'm not trying to make you feel ignorant. I want you to see that I can do this."

She stared at him, more confused now than at any time in their friendship. Her hand drifted toward his and lay on top of it, lovingly her fingers traced the contours of his fingers. Who was this literate Rutger, hiding a knowledge of culture and able to recite lines of novels to her? She closed her eyes and slowly his right hand closed around hers and he pulled it close to him.

"Being in Prestwich ... it's not the place for you," she said.

"Where would be better?" he asked.

"I don't know," she said, "America maybe." She smiled, "San Francisco, I suppose. They must have good universities in San Francisco, yeah?"

"San Francisco'd be better for anyone than Prestwich."

"Maybe."

"I've said things to you tonight, Annabella, that I've never even let myself think about. You know? Like this: there's a scene in the novel *Bonjour Tristesse*, where the main character makes love in a sailboat with a bloke named Cyril. It's beautiful, Cyril is beautiful. What would it be like to make love in a sailboat with a man like Cyril? I never let myself think those things, and now I can stop."

"It's hard being gay in England," she said, "bloody hard, it's all stacked against you. You know that?"

He said nothing.

"Rutger?"

He looked at her. "I don't have to cross that bridge tonight, do I?" The sunlight on Rutger's arm felt warm, felt like a sign of some sort. He ruffled Annabella's wild hair. "You look like something electrical fell in the bath with you. You're a mad woman, you are."

She laughed.

He laughed back.

She looked at him, then she shrugged and smiled. "I've always believed that dreams can come true."

He closed his eyes. "I don't know. It can seem like, you know, life is just dreams and ... imaginings anyway, can't it? All I feel, all I hope for, all I want, that's just the dream of my life and yet it's who I am and it's everything else -- traffic lights, shoes, houses, the hard real world -- that's just dust."

"Just dust ..." she echoed mutedly.

"Yes," he said. A hint of pain gathered softly in his voice, only a hint, but there nonetheless. "Just dust."

"And what side of paradise are you going to live on?"

He smiled. "I don't know much about either side yet, do I?"

"Then you'll have to do something about that, won't you, Mr. I'm-going-to-college-and-be-a-poofter teacher?"

"Yes," he agreed, "I suppose I will." He thought he heard something in her voice, and he asked softly, "Don't you believe me then, Annabella? About being a teacher?"

She shrugged. "It's so sudden like, that's all. And there are so many obstacles."

Yes," he agreed, but not sadly, "there are those."

Although ready for bed, Rutger could not shake off the sensations produced by his conversation and drink with Annabella. Everything seemed odd to him just now. In this life which had long grown accustomed to complacency everything now felt peculiar, unusual. Alone in his room he felt almost elated, as if a warning claxon, which had sounded stridently in his mind for years, telling him to go slowly, be cautious, take care, had finally been turned off. Standing at his window he wanted to laugh at himself. A balm, laughter always made his head clearer. But despite the elation no laughter came from him tonight and -- even if much of his laughter in recent years had been forced -- a lack of laughter was a phenomenon to which he was unused.

Rain thundered down as he climbed into bed and pulled the covers tightly about his neck. He really saw himself as a teacher, saw himself in front of a classroom, smelly whiteboard marker in hand -- but did he so easily see himself with another man, kissing, being kissed, making love? Annabella's face filled his inner vision, her face with its watchful eyes. To what end did she look at him the way she did in the pub? Curiosity? Disbelief? Pity? He sought sleep, but his mind wouldn't be quieted. He recalled a conversation he and Annabella had once, in which she claimed that there were always foreshadowings of significant events. Captains of ships knew in advance that their ship would go down, generals knew they would win outmanned battles, despite odds and statistics.

He sat up. He had a premonition. The thought shot through him like an electrical current, and within seconds he flicked on the light and stood in the center of his room. A premonition of success. He fell into his chair. Wind howled, a tracery of rain tapped lightly on the window. Once again he tried laughter, but the sound of his voice disturbed him. He put his head in his hands. It must all be the beer, or a film he had seen, a story he'd read about in The Guardian. Ordinary North Manchester lads didn't have premonitions.

Those straightforward thoughts began to settle him. Something put him in mind of something else and the chain reaction brought him to the 'premonition.' There could be no forewarning, not of success, not of disaster; a good teacher would say to that emotional extravagance, 'I'm not sure we ought to put much faith in so-called premonitions.' He shook his head and went back to the window. For a long while he watched Manchester wink and blink beneath her watery mantle. That, too, felt also settling. Generally speaking, Manchester had been good to Rutger. Then he climbed back into bed, closed his eyes, and would not open them again for anything.

Because strangest thing of all, he still felt elated.

Kirsten discovered Julian alone at the kitchen table, his head in his hands. Presciently, she had anticipated this sorrowful tableau as she came down the stairs. This, she thought, as a variation on the thoughts she'd had all day, would be her next six months. She lived now with sadness in her house. How could this not affect her husband? Her marriage? Her very sense of self? 'Oh God, Julian,' her heart screamed. 'Why've you done this to us?'

He looked up when she entered the room.

"Can't sleep?" she asked.

"No."

"Jet lag?"

"Maybe." He played with the salt and pepper shakers. "There was an article in the *The Outlook*. Did you know that?"

"No," she said.

"I don't suppose all that many people read it. But I did. It said I was 'rumored' to be despondent, which I guess I was. But it also said this thing that haunts me, Kirsten. I can't stop thinking about it. It said that there were no charges to be brought, which must mean they considered it, the police I mean. They must have considered charging me with murder."

He looked haunted.

Her hand came up to her mouth, an involuntary action. "No, no, manslaughter or negligence or something," she said, as if somehow the precise terminology mattered, "not murder."

He only shrugged.

She went over to him and put her hands on his shoulders, sorrier for him than she could possibly express. "I'm sorry," she said.

The room fell in on itself, utterly quiet. Only England knew how to be this kind of quiet, she thought.

"I got distracted," he said, "by this woman. She'd been stung by a jellyfish. And George, well he was right there beside me. You know? I think he was holding on to my swim trunks even. Then, well," his voice grew hushed. "Then he was gone, and I was responsible."

Again the room's unbearable quiet puffed out round them.

"I'm so unhappy that I'm blind," he said. "I don't see you. Everything's just a cut-out. The world is only cardboard cut-outs. I can see clearly only, well, like only the dark terror of my guilt."

"What can I say to that?" she asked bluntly.

He looked at her and knew no way to express his need for her to reach out to him. If ever he needed anything in his life he needed his sister to reach out and gather him in and hold him safe within her strength. He thought about her question, he thought about words which might mean something to him, but he realized there were no words which offered comfort. Emotions might, touch might, but words were the enemy.

"There really isn't anything you can say," he told her with a shrug. "You don't need to try."

"Is it all right if I just listen?"

"Can you listen if I don't say anything?" he asked.

"Yes, I think so." She sat beside him and held his hand.

They opened themselves to this embracing silence, which plunked like a stone dropped down a well. Kirsten heard the splash. Something dropped into the waters of time, but the identity of that something she found hard to recognize. Perhaps their sense of family, childhood memories, unremembered communications, parents, grandparents, all their shared lives enveloped them. Kirsten felt his pain's measureless immensity. Slowly, by perceptible increments, his head dropped down against her shoulder. Still they were silent. And then, very quietly, he breathed the way a sleeper breathed. He'd fallen asleep on her shoulder. She put her arm around him and kissed his forehead.

"I forgive you," she whispered.

When Kirsten returned to bed she found Alec awake, lying motionless, not even his hands twitching. Turning slightly she saw his eyes open, saw that he stared at the ceiling.

"We'd better talk," she said.

"How's Julian?"

"He's a wraith, Alec, worse than I expected."

"Gone to bed at last?" he asked.

"Yes."

"Good." His face turned toward her. "Kirsten?"

"Alec?"

"Look," he told her. "I'm not trying to be difficult, but there's a principle at stake here. Don't you see that? Having Julian here is wrong; it amounts to taking sides. We don't know the full truth of that day, we never shall. What we know is that George's babysitter allowed him to drown."

She said nothing for a long while. Then slowly, she said, "If I try to understand your feelings then I'll lose touch with my own feelings," she said, "and it's been hell trying to understand my feelings today."

She felt him shift position. His heat diminished. This man cared so much for her.

"How can I help you, lovey" he asked.

What could she say? Did it matter? She rolled close to him, and her body knew instinctively how to fit under his arm and over his leg. With her head on his chest things seemed saner. She lay quietly and listened to his heartbeat.

He relented. "I'm sorry it was hell for you today."

"I'm really confused," she told him.

They lay in their intimate silence.

"Julian desperately wants you to like him again. Can't you see that? He's beside herself trying to figure out how to reach you. Because you're important to me, because we've all known each other for so long, because we're somehow in this thing together."

"What thing?"

"The next six months."

His hand played with her hair. "I've never said I disliked Julian, only that I blame him."

"I know." She inclined her face in the direction of his chin.

The room fell silent, so silent that she heard the potted ivy growing on the fireplace mantle. This silence mirrored the one she experienced half an hour before   with   Julian.

"All these years and I'm still scared of losing you," Kirsten said, starting to crying.

"What? Oh, my darling. You won't lose me. Separation anxiety dominated your childhood. But you're not going to lose me ... never, my love." He pulled her up to him and kissed her. "I love you, Kirsten."

Even after so many years, nothing moved her as Alec's kisses did.

"I love you too," she said, sniffling through her tears

"Shall we test out the myth of the vaginal orgasm?"

"All right," she laughed. "But keep in mind that it's not a timed test."

Brooke made a cartoon-like scream before she dropped the platter of dip and chips. It clattered on the entry hall tiles, dip splattered on the wallpaper, tortilla chips tumbled over the stairs and skittered beneath the desk. In the living room, everyone immediately fell silent. Brooke bent, her back to the gathering, and began picking at the mess. They shouted silly things to her now, meant to be supportive. Of course, they were chiefly drunk and couldn't care less. But Brooke cared; she wouldn't let herself become an object of pity.

"Do you need some help?" one of Wyatt's co-workers asked from behind her.

"No," Brooke said without turning, "I can get it."

The young woman also bent down, but in the way Brooke imagined a high-fashion model bending down, all legs and tightly balanced ass. She picked up a piece of the platter and looked into Brooke's face. "I'm sure you're so not ready for company and still totally upset and ... *everything*," she said.

"No, I'm okay," Brooke said with an unsuccessful attempt at a smile.

The woman gave her a soulful look and held a bit of Brooke's hair away from her face. "Everybody like knows how hard it is," she said. Then, when Brooke offered her no response, said, "I'll go get a sponge and towel. Be right back."

Brooke watched her go into the kitchen.

"Patronizing bitch," she said under her breath.

"You got it under control?" Wyatt asked.

Brooke turned to him. He stood on the step which led down into the living room.

"Don't worry about it," he said.

"Why would I worry about it?" she asked. "Some clueless bimbo's gone to get a sponge and towel."

"It's okay, I mean."

"Of course it's okay," she said, "why wouldn't it be okay? I dropped a platter of fucking plastic chips and fatty dip. And I've slipped on these frigging tiles about a thousand times. Haven't I?"

Without answering, Wyatt reached up and tousled her hair. She felt now as if she were being pitied by the pitiable and she turned furiously away, so that his hand couldn't reach her. More than anything in the world she wanted to be left alone. For an instant she wished she were at a movie theater, watching something .... *avante garde*, new, Italian maybe.

Yesterday afternoon, from where she sat on the upstairs patio of the coffee house, Brooke saw people emerge from the matinee at the cinema below. She watched them laugh, jostle one another, their loud talk filtered up to her like smoke. In particular she focused on a family, mother, father, two boys about ten and seven. With a zoom lens she assessed every gesture, analyzed every nuance of their facial movements, a luxurious torture.

"I love you, Chris," Wyatt said.

"*Jesus.*" She turned back to him. "I will not become an object ... of ... *pity*," she hissed.

"What?"

"I will not be pitied."

Wyatt's co-worker had returned and stood helplessly with a towel in her hand, the third point of a triangle. The sound of a siren warbled away up Pico Boulevard toward Century City.

Brooke placed a piece of broken platter on the desk and, with her back to the woman and Wyatt, calmly flipped through the sheaf of papers and bills there. What did it mean, 'cafe non-alcoholic beverages' for $6.39 on her Nordstrom bill? Strange. Coffee, perhaps? But something else as well. She saw the date, but drew a blank. Brooke's mind had once been a steel trap. No longer. Now she couldn't remember on what and with whom she spent $6.39 at Nordstrom.

She suddenly wheeled around, snatched the towel from the woman's outstretched hand and said with the stab of a vocal stiletto, "There are more goddamned chips in that cupboard above the stove, dear ... and the dip's on the second shelf of the fridge."

Neither the woman nor Wyatt spoke or moved.

"And a glass of chardonnay, perhaps?" Brooke asked Wyatt.

"Sure," he said softly, then looking at his co-worker he added, "some wine?"

"Well, yeah ... I guess," she said. She looked from one to the other and then she went back into the kitchen, presumably to organize more dip and chips.

"Brooke ..." Wyatt started to say.

"*Just leave me the fuck alone,*" she snapped.

They stared a moment.

"My wine?"

"Okay," he said. "Okay."

6

Through his open window, the early-morning air smelled like mown grass, birds sang, shrubbery exploded in green and lavender, Dressing quickly, Julian crept downstairs. In Alec and Kirsten's sunlit suburban corner of England, flowers hung in pots beside the windows, festooned the borders, sprouted from wooden washtubs. Kirsten had gone native; no one in their family had ever encouraged the growing of flowers. Opening the French doors to the garden, he stepped outside. The landscape resembled a woodland into which a tract house had inexplicably inserted itself. Except for the abated noise of a British Airways plane descending into Manchester Airport, the twentieth century hardly intruded at all.

He went to a rhododendron and examined the whitish-pink blossoms. His life now restricted itself to a narrow aperture, past, present, future, all relationships, all experiences, all sensations, thoughts, accomplishments, failures viewed through the aperture of George's death, the entirety of his existence as narrowly focused as a camera lens. As a photographer excluded more than he could include, Julian also excluded more than he could include: happiness, love, freedom. When you killed someone, that happened, he thought.

"You're up early," Alec said from beside him. Julian started. "It doesn't seem early. My inner clock's out of whack."

They looked at one another.

"It's such a beautiful yard," Julian said.

"All these years with Kirsten," Alec smiled, "and I still find it odd to hear my garden described as a yard."

"Whatever it's called, it's beautiful." Julian looked away, and the rising sun made him squint. "I hope this weather holds."

"Unfortunately they're calling for rain."

"Isn't that always the way in England?"

"Not necessarily," Alec said. "Blackpool today, then? Sorry about having to postpone."

"No worries, Alec."

Again they looked at one another and said nothing for a long while.

"How's your family?" Alec asked.

For a moment Julian's voice caught in his throat. He panicked. His squinting eyes were blind with pain. But then he collected himself and said, "Fine. Mom's still bothered a bit with her arthritis, but otherwise they're all okay."

He prayed Alec wouldn't ask him about Wyatt and Brooke. He couldn't bear it.

"Good, good," Alec said. "So, Julian, are your plans for the next six months to remain here?"

"Here?"

"With us? In Manchester?"

"Yes," Julian said. "I think so. I don't know. I hadn't thought about real plans. I've been painting my life with enormous strokes of the brush for the last weeks," Julian said. "Simply leaving home and getting here seemed like an accomplishment. I didn't think I'd make it this far. Never mind. I guess I don't have any real plans, that's what I should say."

"If you're ever interested, my sister Margot and her husband Tony have a smashing flat in Paris, near the Odeon. Really lovely. It's almost always vacant. If you'd like the key, for a week, a weekend, a month even, you've only to ask."

"Thanks," Julian said.

"Something to keep it in mind. Paris could be fun."

Julian nodded. "Trying to get rid of me?"

"Just trying to be ... helpful." Alec looked at his watch. "Mind if I shower first?"

"No, of course not. Rights of ownership and all that."

They looked at one another.

"I didn't mean to be rude," Julian said. "Thanks for offering the flat in Paris."

"It's there if you want it."

Julian looked away, over the fence, toward a cluster of towering oak trees. "Maybe Kirsten will decide to come over with me, we could make it a twosome. She might also enjoy Margot and Tony's smashing flat as well."

Alec looked aghast. He said nothing.

"Thanks again, Alec," Julian said.

"Don't mention it," Alec said back.

Brooke heard Wyatt's footsteps on the basement staircase. When he appeared at the bottom and peered into the murky half-light, she turned away, avoiding him. She heard only his voice, disembodied, unreal.

"What's the story?" he asked. "You're sitting down in the basement now?"

" What do you think is the story?" she demanded, still without looking at him.

"You need to sleep," he said, "take one of those pills Dr. Leitner prescribed. Why not?"

"Sometimes sleep can seem just like death," she said, her voice hushed.

The basement filled with the liquid weight of Wyatt's labored breathing.

"Death?" he asked at last.

His nasty tone of voice startled her. She turned back to him sharply and looked directly into his face. "Sometimes I wish I could stay up forever, Wyatt, and never go to sleep again. There are times in your life," she told him, "when you cling so desperately to your memories that they're like a life raft. If you sleep, it's like you'll wake up and find everything altered, everything changed ... you'll have forgotten."

"You're not feeling any better at all," he said.

"*Better*? What am I? Sick? I'm grieving, you asshole."

They fell silent, he knew he'd said the wrong thing ... again.

"Sometimes I feel like I could kill someone myself," she said thickly. "Someone who has done me a wrong. Why not Julian? Sure, it'll be Julian." She laughed softly. "I'll cut his balls off first and ... What. Oh. Feed them to the dog."

In the silence which followed, Wyatt's breathing again flooded the spider webs and fertilizer bags, washing machine, dryer and hot water tank.

" I wonder if my faggot brother is as good at giving head as I am? If we're similar in that ... maybe we're similarly both murderers too. Huh?"

Yet again they remained quiet.

Wyatt sighed.

"Have you had a single moment in your goddamned worthless life that you'd even begin to call profound, Wyatt?"

"I've always done what I had to do," he said simply.

"Yes," Brooke agreed, "I suppose you have." She rose, stepped over to the old redwood patio bench, climbed on it, looked out the narrow window, and then placed her hands on the glass. "But that's one of the differences between men and women. You," she said, meaning men, "don't understand that people have got to give and give and give to others, especially family. Men like to take and when they do give, they expect some frigging recognition for it."

He came and stood beside her on the bench. "Julian is human," he said, "like us, he's not a monster. It's nicer, of course, to make him a monster. But he can't entirely be blamed for things."

"He should have been punished," Brooke said. "Maybe not blamed, okay, but certainly punished. Murder can't go unpunished. Where would we be? And yet, I guess I can understand why somebody might have a little bit of compassion for a jerk like Julian. He's not evil. He's just ... a murderer."

Wyatt's forehead touched against the glass. "Julian loved George," he said softly, nearly a whisper.

Brooke stepped away from him.

"He did," Wyatt said.

She climbed down from the bench and moved toward the stairs.

"*Brooke?*"

She turned back to him and shrieked, "He *is* evil and I don't have the slightest bit of compassion for him."

Her words echoed off the walls, bounced and bounced and bounced over the entire house, into and out of rooms, downstairs, upstairs, into George's room. She ran up the stairs two at a time. But she stopped in her tracks and turned back around and looked down at him. "*In te, Domine, speravi,*" she said.

"Come again?"

"I have taken refuge in you, Lord. Psalm 31."

He could think of nothing to say. They stared at one another.

In the end he managed to ask, "And have you?"

She shook her head.

"No," he said, "and me neither."

Julian dressed slowly, periodically sipping the tea on his desk. The day had gone cold, swirling sheets of rain pranced over the city. When he finished dressing and went downstairs, Kirsten and Alec waited for him, dressed warmly themselves.

"There you are," Kirsten said

"Here I am," he agreed.

"You look prepared for a magical mystery tour."

"Is going to Blackpool magical?"

"Any journey with me is magical," Alec said with a wink.

"Well, then," Kirsten said, "we're off."

They climbed into the car. Julian in the front seat, Kirsten in back. Alec engaged the gears and the car bolted into traffic. At first they made no effort to converse, simply observing drizzly streets and traffic. Taking the motorway up past the city into the Lancashire countryside, making off through Northern suburbia, they escaped Greater Manchester's congestion.

"Do you remember when we took you to Stonehenge, and you were so miserably disappointed," Kirsten asked.. 'But it's just a pile of rocks, you said.'"

"They charge you to gape at it from behind frayed ropes," Julian said, "kids screaming, Indian ladies' saris bashing you in the face. Maybe I'll do better today."

"They say there was nothing more dangerous than a man without imagination."

"I'm not without imagination."

Kirsten snorted.

"It *is* a pile of rocks," he said, "isn't it?"

"Yes," Alec said, "and the canals of Venice are full of rats and sewage. Life is more than hamburger parlors and designer clothes."

"Am I being patronized now?" Julian asked.

Kirsten sounded embarrassed. "Not at all. I'm merely suggesting that you may have had too much of the ... California good life."

"What on earth is the 'California good life?'"

She leaned forward and looked at him. She had opened her muffler, and the veins in her throat pulsed visibly. "Be sarcastic if you wish. I'm not afraid of sarcasm.."

He watched her, felt the power of her personality and her good nature. No wonder he liked her so much.

"And," she said, snapping her fingers, "mean it."

They sped up the M6 toward Blackpool, with the roar of the motorway, the shriek of Alec's Siouxsie and the Banshees flashdrive and the sounds of him singing to her Siouxsie and the Banshees tape.

99

Julian turned in his seat to look at Kirsten. "Alec wants to send me to Paris. He's offered me the use of Margot and Tony's smashing flat."

"Are you going?"

"No," he said.

Alec turned down Siouxsie. "I bathed naked as the day I was born, in a fountain in Paris, when I was sixteen. We had this completely typical school trip to Paris. We were brats, of course. But aren't all hordes of sixteen year olds? It was scandalous. Half the girls had their brains fucked out by an Italian football team staying in the same hotel, all of these hairy chests and skimpy shorts cackling and marauding like birds-of-prey through the corridors. Half of us simply smoked too many packs of gauloise, disrupted quiet neighborhood streets and took off our clothes in the middle of the night and splashed around in water full of bird shit."

"What was the purpose of this trip?" Kirsten wondered.

"Purpose? I don't know really. Perhaps there was no purpose."

"Well, why did you go?"

"It's a traditional rite of passage. Boarding schools in Surrey have these rites of passage. You know, one's first 'social class defying' grope by the gorgeous young postwoman with the earring -- not an action which interested me much, though I had to admit she was something to behold -- one's first all night food orgy, one's first escape to Brighton by train. I think independent schools should be made illegal, torn apart by earthmovers, leveled, the ground made into cemeteries."

"They can't be that bad," Kirsten said.

"They're worse. I abhor them. In fact, I abhor privately financed education of any sort."

" You're both unbalanced," Kirsten said. She stared at the back of Julian's head.

"Don't tell me you'd consider sending the Metcalf progeny, should there be any," Alec said, "to an public school?"

"I might ... and there will be."

"I thought you said you weren't sure about children."

"Well," Kirsten said, "nature's intervened."

Alec turned off the music. The car fell silent.

As Alec roared past a lorry carrying huge concrete piping, Julian turned toward the back seat. "What?"

"I'm pregnant."

Julian's jaw dropped. He stared at her, horrified. Kirsten had never seen a jaw actually drop. She read about it. Now she saw it.

George, she thought.

George caused Julian's look of horror. He understood now why she didn't rush to his defense, understood that her identification with Brooke grew stronger every day. She should have told Brooke first, he thought. But now \ she must never tell Brooke. She should have her baby in secrecy and Brooke must never know about it, see it, hold it. Having this baby would be like ripping Brooke's heart out and attempting to raise it. She looked again at Alec and on their sister's behalf she hated him. Thank God he would be gone when the baby was born, she didn't want him to see it either. This child would be raised without an American family, without aunts, uncles, grandparents.

"Have you told Alec?" Alec asked.

"No. It's not time yet."

Julian turned in his seat an stared out the front window. "Congratulations."

"Thanks," Kirsten said.

She sat there quietly a moment in the seat. Never had she felt more isolated from life. Perhaps this too quiet place was the real world and other peoples' noisy impertinence wasn't real at all. Why had she never felt this sense of isolation before, a sensation like the peace of meditation or the quietude of prayer? She savored it. She wasn't alienated from Julian and Brooke, they simply remained uninvolved with her, interacting with her but not merging with her. Always in her life she merged with the people around her. She picked up the tone, for instance, of the person with whom she spoke on the phone. Alec always said, 'I heard you talking to so-and-so,' only on the basis of her tone of voice. Sympathetic listening he called it. She sure as hell wasn't a sympathetic listener today.

Alec hit the accelerator, "Let's think of names. Roxanna, now there's a name for you. Strong, feminist, world-conquering. Roxanna."

"We'll have to take our chances on the sex," Kirsten said, "and he or she may even end up going to an independent school, and might just conquer the world, but I can tell you one thing for sure. Male or female, it's damn well *not* going to be named Roxanna."

Mary Clarke, the postgraduate secretary, in a kind of bitchy perpetual motion beneath her fluffy sweater, caught him in the hall. "Oh, Dr. Metcalf, there you are. I thought you must be beavering away in the library."

"No such luck. Postgraduate Research Committee meeting."

"Oh dear," she said like a death knell.

"Yes. It simply gets worse and worse, doesn't it? Today we're scraping for donations to keep ourselves in the black from a semi-literate wanting to research 'those loving poems that we may be discussing in the context of the oracle tradition."

"Oh *dear*."

"Quite," Alec said. "The word I had used was oral, you see."

"Perhaps," she said, in an attempt to cheer him up, "Oracle works better. Is there an oracle tradition?"

"\Presumably. It brings in the funds, doesn't it? Thousands of pounds a year for every overseas post-grad."

"But maybe it's worth it for them, to live in England."

"Looked at student accommodation recently?"

" Well," she said, "student accommodation is one problem we won't solve this afternoon. It's your wife for you, on the telephone. It came through to my desk. I'll transfer it back."

Alec let himself in and sat down behind his desk. The phone rang and he picked it up. "Kirsten?"

"Alec, I've been hanging her forever. I'm calling from a silly shop."

"I was in a postgraduate research committee meeting. Mary Clarke's just found me."

"She's probably been burbling away to you in the hall, flouncing and trouncing in her fluffy sweater. She's in love with you."

"Of course she's not," he said.

"Don't sound so guilty then."

"I'm sure I don't sound guilty." He listened to the roar of a lorry as it shook the store. "Is there a problem?"

"I shouldn't have blurted I'm pregnant out in the car, with Julian more or less trapped ... in so many ways, if you think about ... no, no," she said obviously to a server, "I'm just having a browse. Yes, yes,   I   will.."

"Kirsten, it's marvelous that you're pregnant, Julian or nor Julian, trapped or free as a bird."

Her sin, she saw, was forgivable.

"Let's go out tonight," he said. "The two of us. Let's celebrate."

She faltered for a moment and only in that moment her lips nearly formed the words 'what about Julian?' The quiet isolation returned. Even from Alec, whom she loved, she felt detached, her entire being focused upon something new inside of her. Did she even care about Julian, she wondered? Why should she feel compelled to play the good hostess to this murdering brother, unworthy of her concern. Let him eat fish fingers and frozen Tesco oven chips on his own."

"Yes," she finally said, "Let's. Can you make the reservations?   Is the Marketplace all right?"

"I'm so happy, Kirsten, really, I'm so very happy."

He sounded happy; he sounded as happy as she'd ever heard him.

"Me too," she said.

"You don't sound it.   Are you sure everything's all right."

"Yes. Of course. It's just being on my phone in a shop."

He tried to persuade her again that she sounded troubled, she tried again to persuade him she wasn't. They rang off. How could she be a mother, she wondered, lost in this sea of unhappiness, her sister and her brother unknown to her? And for herself, she just plain felt worthless. No child could love her. Perhaps her baby too would die horribly, perhaps this time it wouldn't be Julian's fault, perhaps this time it would be her fault.

She leaned her head against a rack of clothes. Her panic felt acute. A contradictory swirl of emotions engulfed her, a sense of waiting, but knowing that she waited for nothing. For a moment she saw herself within a bag, stitched shut, unopenable, then that moment passed and she saw herself in an ever-expanding universe without boundaries. Within her anxiety no hope existed, small or large, dark or light, no hope, no light. Then she realized that Julian lived this way continually and that realization felt inexpressibly horrible. No part of her wanted to understand that in this emotional fire storm her brother struggled day in and day out. She cried then, and her tears ran into her mouth, she tasted them, salty, personal, her tears. She wanted Alec, then she didn't want Alec, her baby thrilled her and then her baby depressed her.

'Help me,' she said silently, to no one at all.

Then she fainted.

Alec stared at the phone, replaying the conversation. Kirsten's voice held something odd in. What? Simple attack of nerves? As always, anxiety gripped him when things went wrong with Kirsten. He cupped his head a moment in his hands. Then he did something which seemed completely natural. He found the telephone number and phoned Kirsten's parents in California. This should be welcome news to them, something to offset the pain of George's death: an English grandchild, a new grandchild.

"Hello?" Kirsten's mother said.

"Nadine? This is Alec."

"Oh, hi, Alec. It's Alec," she said, presumably to Kirsten's father. "How are you?"

"Good thanks."

"Did Julian arrive safely?"

"Yes. All in one piece, Kirsten and J have taken him to Blackpool for the day. It's a seaside resort, north of here."

"We know where Blackpool is, dear."

"Yes. Sorry."

"That's good."

"What? That I'm sorry."

"No, no, that he's getting out."

"Oh. Right. Listen, I'm ringing to pass on some news. Kirsten's pregnant."

The phone line hissed in an awful silence before Nadine said, "Why that's just wonderful, Alec. Here, let me put Eddie on. Eddie," she shrieked. "Eddie, get in here. Just a minute," she said to Alec.

The phone fumbled between hands.

"Hi, Alec," Eddie said.

"Hello. I was just telling Nadine that Kirsten's pregnant."

"Super," Eddie said. Eddie, at least, didn't miss a beat. "Is she there?"

"No, I'm phoning from my office," Alec's stomach sank. Where were the cartwheels? Did it make them realize they'd always be minus their first grandson, the curly headed blond boy they adored? He considered the possibility then that he shouldn't have phoned presumptuously like this. He'd done something wrong, something which would make Kirsten furious. Kirsten should have phoned them. He'd usurped her family privilege. He'd made a mess.

"Alec?" Eddie asked. "Are you still there?"

"Yes."

"Well, thanks for letting us know," Eddie said.

"I rang you first, before Julian said anything."

"Good of you."

Could he persuade them to forget he even rang, Alec wondered. "I'll have Kirsten ring you ... " he stopped himself from saying 'tonight.' Belatedly he tried to put the ball back in Kirsten's court.

Nadine returned to the line. "Thanks so much for   calling,   Alec."

"It's always   pleasant to talk with you." Pleasant? He was making it worse, he thought.

"You know, things haven't been so good on this side of the Atlantic," Nadine said. "I guess you understand why."

"How are Wyatt and Brooke?"

"Honest   answer?"   she   said.   "Worse."

"In what way?"

"Wyatt just can't snap out of it, he's drifting farther and farther away from us. He's just filled all the way up with some kind of elemental pain, complete and primal. I can hardly bear to see it."

"It's hell to lose a child," Alec said limply. But what did you say?

"Amen to that," Nadine told him.

"And Brooke? How's she?" Alec asked.

"She puts on a better face. But that's all it is, a face she puts on."

"I can't tell you how sorry we are," Alec said.

"I can tell you one thing, it's damn well going to tear this family apart," Nadine said. Her voice squealed down the phone line like winter wind.

Had Alec caused this? With his fool's errand of a phone call?

"I don't perceive Julian to be doing well either, you know," Alec said.

What was he doing now, he asked himself? Defending the murderer?

"Of course not," she said with loyal maternal immediacy, "I said the family and I meant him too. We've all worried a great deal about Julian. It must be excruciating for him."

"Can we do anything for Brooke and Wyatt?"

"You're doing it already."

"How's that?"

"Keeping Julian over there in England for six months. Hell," Nadine said, as if unaware of the contradiction with her maternal protectiveness of a moment before, "keep him a year. That'd be better. Keep him forever."

"Don't think we're up to that."

"I wasn't serious," she ssaid softly. "Of course not."

Again it fell silent, a large and distinctly pained silence.

"Work beckons," Alec said, "I'd better go. Nice talking to you."

"Yes," Nadine said, "Very nice. And thanks again for this ... wonderful, wonderful news. Bye, Alec."

"Bye," Alec said, and the forlorn notes of his

voice seemed to hang there on the line before he heard the click.

7

Dim light diffused in the thick pub air, obscured by clouds of stale smoke. Music blared from a CD-playing jukebox, Saturday night sounds pierced the walls, the landlord's voice boomed across the room. Rutger and his mates, young men he'd known since school, sat around a table. But Rutger, the sometimes life of the party, stayed uncharacteristically quiet, tucked away in the corner, grey eyes withdrawn behind their lashes. And no one bothered him, his thoughts were his own. His mates, after all, understood him. But his friend Alec's sister Helen, dressed to her finest and wafting perfume in her wake, sat down next to him, her eyes on the door, where she watched for her boyfriend, late from a cricket match.

"You're fucking lovely you are, Rutger Whitaker," she said. "Sheila Hargrave and I are over there watching you and getting wet we are. Isn't he?" she asked the men.

"Isn't he what?"

"Isn't he fucking lovely?"

"Fucking lovely, heck," one of them said, "he's got a right mood on tonight, does Rutger."

"I don't," Rutger protested, "I'm only tired."

"No, he's fucking lovely." She pushed his hair off his forehead. "Restless but fine, like high quality marble."

Rutger smiled. "Fancy a pint?" he asked her.

"We're going out to eat, aren't we, if he ever fucking gets here. Thanks anyway, love." tossed her hair, and asked Rutger, "Sitting all alone with this lot on Saturday night when you're so fucking hunky you could have any girl in Prestwich. Are you a candidate for the priesthood, then?"

"I'm not Catholic, am I?"

The girl laughed loudly, exposing her teeth, enjoying herself immensely. She covered her mouth with one hand, looked coyly over the top of her fingers at him, and then she laughed again. "I'm wondering if some spider hasn't already spun her web round you, one of those hoity-toity bitches you work with in Manchester. Ooh, I tried to go shopping in their t'other day and some big-bummed tart of a bitch chased me right out."

Not a bad description of Pamela, Rutger thought.

"Has she then, some spider, spun a web?"

"If she has, I don't know about it."

"If she's a truly crafty bitch you won't know it, will you? She'd fucking make it feel like lace when it's really steel."

Rutger laughed.

"Hey, she's getting rid of his mood, she is," one of the men said, "She's got him laughing and all."

She leaned close and whispered into Rutger's ear. "You're a cut above these buggers, lovey, aren't you?"

Rutger said nothing.

"Fuck 'em, I say, don't let them hold you back. If you need to move on, you fucking move on. Our Alan did, lives in London now, has a big flat in Shepherd's Bush, I went to visit him last Boxing Day and I was gob-struck. He's done all right, has Alan." She squeezed his thigh. "You hear me?"

He nodded.

"You know for Spain his Lordship's made me buy a fucking purple florescent dental floss bikini," she said, referring to her still absent boyfriend, "and I said they've fucking gone out of fashion, I read it right in *Cosmopolitan*, and he said, 'I won't be pointing

112

Percy at *Cosmopolitan*, will I? Oh, he's low he is, low."

They all laughed then, even Rutger.

Water drowned him. He always kept it too hot. Rutger loved the torrents of hot water, washing over his head, over his shoulders, down the length of him, washing away sins, the gurgle of life and death as water ran up his nose, down his throat. Then, too quickly, he dressed and ran out of the house, a piece of toast in one hand, a banana in the other. He scoffed them on the way to the Prestwich Metrolink station, abandoning the banana skin in an overflowing rubbish bin in the Sainsbury's carpark.

He rushed up the ramp to the platform, drawing a hand through his still wet hair. Several months ago he came up with a manic-depressive theory, which held that taking the bus meant depression and taking the train meant elation. In other words, the essentially subconscious action of whether he turned left for the train or right for the bus revealed his mood. Never mind the forty pence fare difference, and never mind that for other people transport was serendipity. Well, here he stood on the train platform. Serendipitous or portentous? Maybe he simply felt pleased his mum had gone to London, maybe it merely pleased him to have the house to himself. A rare event, having an entire house to himself.

No. More to it, he thought, always more to his moods.

The metrolink tram tooted into the station, he pressed the button which said 'press when illuminated,' boarded and found a seat. Unlike the bus, this time of morning a socially diverse crowd rode the train: everyone from students to business types in suits, well-dressed suburban matrons from Whitefield and Bury with their Margaret Thatcher purses for a day's shopping in the city center. Bus riders tended more uniformly to be at the lower end of the socioeconomic ladder. So it couldn't merely be serendipity, could it? With whom did he identify more? The business types and suburban matrons, or the people on the bus whose income more closely duplicated his?

Perhaps for the first time Rutger considered his lack of social consciousness. Why did he so rarely think about where he fit on the social scale? He knew it said something about him, knew it spoke to his self-absorption, or his alienation, or his sense of being 'different.' An outsider, always an *uitlander*, his place, no place. Suddenly, sitting there on the metrolink, considering his lack of class identification, his dream of being a teacher returned full force.

He turned his face to the window and watched the urban landscape of Cheetham Hill, these windswept hillsides a world away from the golf course and church he and Annabella visited in Didsbury. This wasn't upwardly mobile South Manchester. Not particularly inspiring Cheetham Hill. But then, if you paid attention, what might you see that others miss? The almost poetic undulation of identical rooftops? The curious juxtaposition of an oak tree and the burned out faces of abandoned council flats? A pretty mother in a flimsy pink blouse pushing her baby in a pram, holding the hand of a little blond boy in trousers which didn't fit him?

The way a policeman stood casually beneath a logo reading, 'death to the genocidal fascist police murderers?'

He noticed the businessman across the aisle from him. "Got a lot to recommend it, does Cheetham Hill," Rutger said. "Look at it." He gestured out the window. "I mean, they're really living out there."

"Out where?"

"In Cheetham Hill." Rutger looked away from the businessman, who thought it all a send up, and peered out the window again. "In Cheetham Hill," he said, but this time so quietly that only he heard the words.

"What a charming thought," the businessman said.

"You have to make the best of what's offered you in life."

"Sad isn't it?

"No, no it's not, that's my point," Rutger said.

Rutger felt the businessman's eyes on him, scornful perhaps, looking through him as if he -- like the people of Cheetham Hill -- were transparent.

But the businessman shrugged in acquiescence, a moment of truth, dexterous but also manipulative. They both looked out the window again, but the vista had already changed, the train well beyond Cheetham Hill.

"I suppose it's all as it should be really," the businessman said.

"Now *that*," Rutger said, "is sad."

Julian and Kirsten were taking a day trip to Liverpool, but the trip had started out with her being sick and then the train arrived late and – not quite a surprise – they found they had nothing to talk about.

He looked out the window and saw lines of sleety rain, and he felt desolate.

She also turned her head and looked out the window. Out of the corner of her eye she saw that his eyes were closed, his head thrown back against the seat. They still made no effort to talk. The trip proceeded south through Lancashire and neither spoke through several stops and starts. Rain splashed against the window.

"I can't bring him back," Julian suddenly said.

Kirsten saw his eyes were still closed. She grew determined not to indulge him anymore, no longer to contribute to his self-pity. She returned her gaze out the window, with contemptuous scowl.

Where could he go, Julian wonderered, if he were to leave Kirsten and Alec? Unwelcome anywhere. He had some money saved up. Kirsten hadn't looked at him yet, as if he didn't exist. Perhaps he didn't; perhaps he shouldn't. It didn't matter where he went. Why not India? He could ingest liver flukes, turn jaundiced, vomit blood. That might feel like repentance. Landscape passed by the train window. He looked at Kirsten and struggled for the words that would express it all, for the words that would sum things up. What were those words? They funneled down his brain, words and words and words and none of them seemed the least bit right.

She turned and saw that his eyes swelled with tears. "I'm not going to talk about this anymore," she said. "I mean I *won't* talk about it anymore. Not for a while. I need to think. I need to think about how I feel. I'm so goddamned aware of how everyone else feels, how you feel and Brooke and Alec and mom and dad and goddamned everybody else. I want to think about how I feel for a while."

"You told me it wasn't my fault. Was that just a lie? Was that what you felt or not?"

"Look," she said, "Don't damn well bring George's death up any more. That's what I'm saying. Okay?"

He nodded, but not at her, to himself. The train stopped in a place called Bolton and Julian stood up, his face flushed. "No," he said, "it's not 'okay.' Because it was an *accident*, that's what George's death was, an *accident*. I didn't do anything. *I'm not a criminal*. I'm a victim of circumstance. How do you think you'd feel if you were me? And don't say you wouldn't have taken your eyes off George if you were me, because you don't know that. And until you acknowledge the fact that I'm a victim too ... well, there's just not a hell of a lot for us to say to one another."

"Julian ..."

He glared at her, cutting her off with the words, "You know, I want to tell you that I think you .. all of you, mom, dad, Alec, Chris, Wyatt ... are unspeakably cruel to me." He strode down the corridor, pushed the button, opened the door and got off the train. Behind him he heard the train start to move again. When he turned around he looked straight into Kirsten's shocked white face. For an instant he thought he would scream. He felt it well up from some deep, ugly place inside him, scratch at his throat, struggle to get free. Tentacles of scream nearly emerged from his mouth, scream fingernails tore at his lips. But he swallowed them, tentacles, nails, beak of scream, like a coiled snake the scream thrashed in his gut.

Then he turned away from Kirsten, sprinted toward the station exit and disappeared.

Unfamiliar with Bolton, Julian simply followed the 'way out' signs. Across from the station a cafe lit up the soggy pavement, and he went there. A friend of his at college once said, 'Treat airplanes like flying bars and in strange cities always go first to a restaurant. Waiters know everything.' Julian ordered coffee from the waitress and sat at a table by the window.

Sure, everybody wanted George alive. What could he have done? The jellyfish had terrified the lady, he told George to stay right there beside him. George shouldn't have wandered off. The accident happened because he defied instructions and wandered off from the adult who watched him. Hell, Julian thought, I'd give my right arm if it would bring George back. But all the right arms in the world, stacked together in a tower that touched the sky, wouldn't bring him back. It could have been Wyatt there with him at the beach, it could have been his grandfather, it could even have been high-and-mighty Alec Metcalf.

His coffee arrived. As he sipped it, the steam felt good against his face. Given his druthers he'd leave England today, disappear, but unfortunately he'd left his clothes, travelers cheques and passport in Didsbury. He finished the coffee, wishing he could exist without a family, exist independently, be an island. He stood up and gestured for the bill. When the waitress brought it he paid and went out to the street. For some time he wandered aimlessly, went in and out of several stores, until he saw the recognizably clean storefront of a national clothing chain and went in. He climbed upstairs to the men's wear section. As he rummaged through a pile of socks a sales clerk came up beside him and asked if he could help.

Julian turned.

He and the clerk looked at each other in confused recognition.

Then Julian said, "Didsbury."

"*Didsbury?*"

"That church," Julian said. "My sister and I were visiting it. You were there with someone else."

"Oh, yes, that's right," Rutger said. "I knew I recognized you."

"You work here?" Julian said, in evident surprise.

Rutger noted the surprise and said with a shrug, "Yes and no. I work for the same store, or one of the same stores, in Manchester. But I got sent out to Bolton today because half the store phoned in sick."

"Are they on strike or something?"

"No. Just the Bolton climate, I imagine."

They stared at each other.

"Maybe I should ask you what you're doing here," Rutger said.

"Long story," Julian said.

Rutger waved his hand around the store. "I'm not exactly overworked like."

"I was on a train, with my sister Kirsten. We had a fight and I was so pissed off that I got up and walked away. Turns out I was here, in this place."

"Bolton." Rutger said. "Must have been some fight."

"That's the long story part of it."

Julian leaned back against the rail and looked into Rutger's curious eyes. He told him the story, leaving nothing out, describing to this stranger every sensation, from the horrible first moments to sitting with the police divers on the breakwater after midnight as they continued searching for the body. He told Rutger that his family thought him a murderer.

When Julian finished, Rutger remained silent. For several long moments he could think of nothing to say, every feeling to which he had himself given in, every one of his own miseries faded away into insignificance. "I'm sorry," he finally offered, "about them blaming you like."

"There was even some idiot article in the paper, which mentioned the police, about how they'd examined the case for negligence, something like that. It was a big fucking deal." He blinked away tears. "Why am I telling you this? You don't want to hear it. God. I should check myself into a hospital or something."

Though a difficult thing for him to do, Rutger extended his hand and held Julian's upper arm. Rutger's family rarely offered physical comfort. Rutger didn't embrace his own mother when his father died, neither did she embrace him. To offer such comfort to someone essentially a stranger represented a quantum leap. But a leap toward what?

Julian looked away. "I guess you asked."

"I guess I did."

"And it just felt, there on the train, like I couldn't take any more," Julian said. "It was too much, more than I could absorb. You see, my sister's pregnant, and it's ... causing this revulsion in her for me. She's worried that I'll kill her baby too."

"You shouldn't say that," Rutger told him, removing his hand from Julian's arm. "You can make something seem true, which is nearly the same thing, I reckon, as it actually being true."

Julian thought about that and again they looked at one another.

"Have some coffee." Rutger said, gesturing toward a chair by the stairs.

"I don't know."

"Sure. Sit like."

"No," Julian said. "Thanks. But I've got to go. I shouldn't have stood here and blathered all this shit. I feel stupid." He made a pretense out of looking at his watch. "I need to move on."

"We talked," Rutger said. "You didn't blather."

Julian went down the stairs. Rutger watched him go. Then Rutger walked to the glass front of the building, where he caught a fleeting glimpse of Julian's jacket as its wearer ran across the street and into an arcade.

The crossing this rainy night proved rough, the nearly empty boat haunted by a broken jukebox playing the same song over and over again. Childish to take the ferry to the Isle of Man, he regretted it now. But it seemed imperative that he get away, as if movement meant action. It didn't. He watched a young woman for a moment, asleep on a bank of chairs, and then he went out on the blisteringly cold deck. Ice pellets like steel struck him, he closed his eyes and listened to the wind and the engines, and when he reopened them the dark sleet struck him blind again. Still he stood there, trying to gaze out on the heaving water, listening. Tears may have filled his eyes, he wasn't certain, and they may have been from the cold rather than emotion.

Things had not gone as he hoped, and not as everyone predicted. If he went to England he'd improve, that's what everyone said. They probably just wanted to get rid of him. He stepped to the rail and this time he knew they were tears. He killed George, the only person to whom he'd ever been indispensable. How could that have happened? How? Before boarding the ferry he phoned Brooke and Wyatt's house and Brooke answered. The very sound of her voice chilled him. Though Julian tried to speak he could not. For several seconds Brooke tried to discover the caller's identity, then she screamed -- actually screamed, he thought, like a scene from Psycho -- and then she slammed the receiver down. Something in that slam connected so powerfully to him, as if she knew it were Julian, somehow sensed his presence there amid the electrical impulses and stray static noises.

Oh, God, why did George die, leaving them all lost, unloved, and forever abandoned? Julian wished he could wave a wand and set back the hands of time. Someone, he couldn't remember who now, told him that time healed all wounds, that normality would at some point return. How patient must he be? How long must they all wait? Perhaps normality would never again return, perhaps Julian had destroyed all their lives and nothing could ever be normal again. He cried, his head hanging low over the railing, his hair soaked and heavy in the wind. He wished he had not loved George so much, because it seemed inexpressibly horrible to have killed the person he loved most in all the world.

Little George, so strong and whole and eager to tackle the future, bright, inquisitive, cheeky, full of enthusiasm, everything people hoped for in a child, until his uncle let him drown. Julian returned to the saloon. Something happened to him, but he didn't know what. For a long string of open-ended minutes he stared across the room and moved with the vibrations of the ship. Something definitely happened to him, something over which he had no control. He gasped and covered his mouth, as if to disguise the noise as a yawn. He lost all his fixed coordinates, he fell free and drifted in a liquid void, without love or family or a stable place to call home. His clenched hands turned white, his breath shallow, pained.

He wondered what happened to him and when it would end.

When they docked he bought another ticket and immediately returned to Liverpool, and then he caught the first train to Manchester.

A leafy summer's evening, a pungent odor from someone's barbecue filling the air, Didsbury's growing shadows cloaked him, silently separated him from other, normal people. He stood on the pavement and watched the traffic. A mauve haze grew around a streetlight as it came on, like a religious aura, refracting off the pavement. He moved up the walk. Music came to him from within the house and he knocked loudly, the knock echoing in his mind, dispelling his many thoughts like cigarettes snubbed out with a hiss. He waited, the music stopped, a few moments later the door opened, warm air rushed out, and Kirsten faced him.

"Hey," he said, then, "I hope you're expecting me."

She wore no make-up and fresh color rouged her cheeks. Her eyes glittered, a hand came up and tucked a strand of loose hair behind her ear.

"Can I come in, Kirsten?"

"Yes, of course. Sorry."

She motioned him into the hall, which smelled deliciously of baking bread. He went into the lounge and sat with a sigh, fingers massaging his temples as if he had a headache. Kirsten stood in the doorway and watched him. The color on her cheeks had begun to glow.

"I tried to go to the Isle of Man, but I turned around once I got there and come straight back to Manchester. I stayed in a hotel last night, but I ... well, I'm back, in one piece."

"I've been worried sick," she said.

"I'm sorry." He looked up. "Can I have something to drink, please. Just a glass of water."

She stared at him a moment longer, then broke her gaze and hurried off. Water ran, then she came back with a tall glass of water, which he finished in one long gulp. He put the glass down on the side table and they regarded one another. A clock ticked loudly.

"You know, Kirsten, I think we've missed the same opportunities in life," he said.

She looked startled. "What opportunities?"

"To be well adjusted, something in our family, I don't know what, it's like we were fed on the same lies, and now we're as we are, all unhappy and twisted."

"We weren't like that before George died."

"Yeah," he said, "we were."

Silently she thought and then she said softly, "Remember the time I ran away?"

"They found you at the airport."

"I wanted to be found," she said. "You can't erase the past, any of it," she whispered, "that's the problem. I talked to you once, Julian, in San Diego, when we were on vacation? When I was sixteen?"

"I remember. You thought you were in love. His name was Joe, he wanted to be a cowboy or something."

"Ride in the rodeo, his family had horses. He was a jerk, you know you get these weird infatuations when you're sixteen, but you were terribly sweet about it. I've often wished it could be like that again. But life's not about cozy little chats in San Diego hotel rooms."

"I was wrong, you know, about you being cruel. You're not."

"Come to dinner with us," she offered. "There's a great new Indian place in Rusholme, they do absolute wonders with dog meat."

"That would be nice," he said. "I've been craving dog meat."

8

Julian awoke in the cold heart of night. Frigid silence enveloped him. The digital clock's reddish glow illuminated the nightstand. He saw his watch and money clip. He felt naked, alone, and of course he thought of George. Frustration throttled Julian. He noticed that he had taken to holding his pillow in his arms. Poor substitution for a real body, it helped him sleep. Moonlight barely picked its way into his room. For some reason, tonight, Julian' loneliness shamed him. He closed his eyes and lay still, but sleep proved elusive. He turned on the light and sat up.

The real hell of his life, he thought, lay in the lack of a safe place. Everything held some fragrance of his guilt. He climbed unsteadily from bed, pulled on his pants, and went downstairs to the kitchen. On the way down, from the window on the landing, he saw the green neon light of an Indian take-away. It seemed to mock his self-indulgence. He leaned on the bannister and took a draw on that neon light, like a cigarette. It helped some, a taste of normality, not much more. He went the rest of the way downstairs and turned on the kitchen lights. Each sleepless three a.m. was the same as the last.

He poured himself a glass of orange juice.

For the first time in his life, perhaps, he noticed the little hairs on his knuckles. They must have been there all along. Mustn't they? He couldn't have grown them as a sign of shame, though he liked the idea, liked thinking of himself as a shamed and degraded werewolf, slinking through the night searching for babies to kill. He slugged back the juice, leaned his head against the window, and closed his eyes. Cold arced through him. He felt pulled down a river, lost, out of his canoe, tossed through rapids, his head barely above the water. A thundering waterfall lay straight ahead, he knew it, he felt the suction draw him toward destruction.

In the still, early hours of morning Julian heard Kirsten move about downstairs in the lounge. Something painful and yet expectant about her sleeplessness made him wonder what she thought about, and if she could in any way sense the future. Sometimes women could. Julian had no prophetic powers himself, but he thought he knew something about Kirsten and her future, and about her unborn child, though he also knew it would be silly to share his gift of sight with her. She would discover things in her own time, her skills at parenting, her depth, her qualities of character. Having a baby might force the pace, it often did, but it was no more than a spray which insured that the blossom set fruit, inevitable in any case.

The first spikey bits of too-early dawn spread over the horizon. Perhaps Kirsten awaited this new dawn so impatiently downstairs. He also rose, then, and went to the window, where the pastoral beauty of sleeping England stretched beneath the inquisitive glow of an immature morning. The air filled with whistling humidity as warm as a lover's breath. A portent, perhaps? Kirsten, too, may have sensed it.

The lounge had fallen quiet.

9

On a cloudless summer eve, men spilled out
on the paving stones between the front of the pub and
a not quite derelict canal. Music and nervous loud
laughter seeped through open windows, buses
streamed down one street, an ambulance blue-lighted
its way along another. Julian stood against the
parapet overlooking the canal, with his back to the
water and his face to the pub, sipping a pint of lager.
Around them soared Manchester's blank-faced 1960s
skyline. He looked to his left, where a man had taken
up a place along the wall with his back to Julian,
shuffling nervously. First he put his foot in one
position, looking aggressive, then he moved it closer
in and looked timid.

He turned his head around. "Hello."

"Hi," Julian said in a startled voice.

"How are things in Didsbury?"

In what he hoped was a more normal
conversational tone, Julian said, "Didsbury's not
exactly a happening kind of place." Then letting a
beat or two pass he said, "I didn't, well, I, you know
..."

"I am," Rutger said.

They stared silently and the silence seemed to
extend itself, as they looked at one another and said
nothing. Julian felt invisible and yet exposed. When
he looked away from Rutger he leaned his head back,
and the sky, as he gazed up into it, reminded him of
things he long forgotten. He remembered the 'jelly
bean' dress his mother wore when he was little, a
Doris Day sack of crumpled velvet ringed with hard
buttony objects like jelly beans all along the bottom.
To his five year old eyes she'd seemed extraordinarily
lovely in it. 'Wear the jelly bean dress,' he used to
say. Particularly he recalled a night when she came

into his room wearing that dress. She kissed him goodnight before going out, and the rush of perfume, the rustle of fabric, the feel of the jelly beans formed a perfect childhood memory.

"I've never been here before," Rutger said. "In fact I've never been to any gay place before." He laughed, and nervous disbelief surfaced both in his laugh and in his words. "I've known about these places, but I've never actually been, only driven by. Once last summer I came back from the cinema this way and looked at all the men. Tonight I came out."

"Farewell the closet?"

"I meant came out to this pub."

"Just my feeble stab at humor," Julian said. When he looked again at the herd of men in front of the pub, he thought this: if he'd been as old when he asked mom to wear the jelly bean dress as George when he died, then George must have had similar impressions, must have held lovely impressions of Brooke, like flies in amber, impressions of an even more resonant purity because of the closeness of the action and the memory. And those impressions were gone forever, with all the other hopes, dreams, aspirations and desires of that one life.

"It must have been hard," he said, referring to Rutger's decision to come to a gay bar.

"Like the fucking Bataan death march," Rutger said. "I turned back three times. I got all the way back to Piccadilly and then I stood there and let two Bury trains go by."

"You wanted to do this."

"I must have."

Julian looked around. "It's pretty harmless really."

"Hard to measure harm," Rutger said.

They smiled at each other in understanding. Julian hadn't guessed about him for a moment, it was like discovering his favorite high school teacher in the men's room of Oil Can Harry's. That happened once.

"I don't know your name," Rutger said.

"Julian."

"I'm Rutger."

It was quiet a moment.

"Been out any more to ... what's the place called?" Julian asked.

"Bolton. No, they've been keeping me closer to home like. How about you? Feeling any better?"

"Not really," Julian said. "Well, actually, this *is* me being better. Two months ago I couldn't even get out of bed. Really. I stayed under the covers until two in the afternoon, kept my robe on and then went back to bed at six."

"Frightening like."

"Felt good at the time. Like being back in the womb."

"Back in the womb," Rutger repeated quietly, "I've never been depressed ... at least not like that."

"You're lucky."

"In some ways."

"Do you want another drink?" Julian asked.

Rutger held up his nearly empty glass and the veins in his arms stood out prominently. "Nerves," he said, "I ought to be careful. It's the kind of night when I could easily drink too much."

"One more won't hurt," Julian said.

"Think not?" Rutger said, but then he smiled, "Sure. Pint of bitter. Thanks."

When Julian returned with the drinks, a curly-headed smiling student type spoke with Rutger. Rutger nodded to Julian, took his drink as he introduced him to Derek. "Julian is American," he said and Derek's eyes brightened. Julian looked at Rutger who, in the interlude of distraction provided by Derek's appraisal of Julian, shrugged helplessly. Derek, obviously deciding that American or not Julian wasn't his type, turned his eyes back to Rutger. The three of them talk about inanities. Finally, Derek said his goodbyes, held on to Rutger's hand too long, nailed him with meaningful eye contact and then went over to a group of his friends.

"Cute bloke," Rutger said.

"Yes," Julian said.

"Friendly."

"Oh yes. Friendly. They're always friendly."

Rutger looked puzzled.

They remained quiet. The crush of men forced them to stand close together. Julian let his arm push against Rutger's chest, his leg touched Rutger's leg. Did he even notice, he wondered?

"Have you had a lot of experience, then?" Rutger asked.

Julian pulled his leg away. "Not really. Several boyfriends. I loved Brian, he was my last."

"You didn't love the others?"

"I don't think so. Maybe Geoffrey ... a little bit."

Rutger thought about that a moment. "Why'd you and this ... Brian bloke split up?"

"He said he needed more space to be himself, whatever that means."

"Probably a lot to him."

132

For the first time, Julian considered that very real possible. He looked at Rutger and thought ... with some terror ... that he so needed a man in his life like Rutger, that he was developing the most intense crush. Even his harsh South African accent turned him upside down with ... well, incipient love? "We kind of jumped into bed before we had time to consider our feelings, then we liked what we did after we jumped into bed and we just kept on doing it until we ... were a couple."

"He didn't love you back?"

"He said he did."

"Was he lying?" Rutger asked.

Julian looked at Rutger. "Most likely."

"I'm sorry," Rutger said, "you've had a lot go wrong like, haven't you?"

They fell quiet again, and stayed that while a long while.

"Want to go somewhere else, or stay here?" Rutger asked, sealing the bargain that they would stay with one another for the evening – at least.

"I don't know the scene in Manchester," Julian said.

They looked at one another comfortably.

"Let's stay here then," Rutger said.

The crowd thinned out, the evening grew colder. Music still pounded through the open windows, but the lights had been turned on inside. Last orders were filled. Curly-headed Derek still remained, standing now by the stained glass windows under frou-frou awnings, his eyes fixed intensely on

Rutger. Julian drifted, in that intoxicated state of self-awareness which couldn't be called drunkenness but was a far cry from sobriety. He felt alternately too aware of Rutger and then too aware of incidental sensory impressions like the feel of the night air, the touch of the breeze, the smell of diesel exhaust from the buses on Princess Street. His head began to hurt.

"Something wrong?" Rutger said.

Julian shook his head.

"Want to have a look?" Rutger nodded his head toward the canal.

"Sure."

Rutger led the way along the wall, up the stairs, across the canal, and then down the dark stairs to the other side. Water trickled through the doors of the lock. It smelled mossy, litter was strewn about, a broken bench straddled a paved area between two bollards, where canal boats tied up while waiting for the locks to open. They stood quietly and looked at the water, which glistened with oily impatience. Suddenly, altogether unexpectedly, Rutger took Julian's hand and held it tightly, bringing it up to his own face and holding it against his cheek. Julian thrilled to the bristle of Rutger's five o'clock shadow, the cool heat of his skin. One of his fingers brushed Rutger's hair. Somehow time stood still. Then Rutger leaned toward him and they kissed.

"You've got a ... great chest," Julian said.

"Thanks," Rutger said back.

Julian clung to Rutger, and then he started crying.

Worse than crying, his insides spilled out.

He cried and he clung, fearing to be let go of, and his tears wet through Rutger's white shirt, revealing dark chest hair like a shadow above his heart. "I'm sorry," he said.

"Don't be."

Rutger kissed Julian' forehead.

But now he held crying Julian and said softly, "Hey, it's all right, man."

"I want to go home with you," Julian said.

"Why do you want to come home with me?"

Julian held Rutger's hand so that the fingers brushed against his lips. "I want you to make love to me."

Rutger said quietly, ""Why?"

"Because you're a man who moves me deeply .. and makes me feel safe." Julian's head hurt again. For emphasis he placed against Rutger's chest. It moved flat and felt Rutger's heartbeat.

Rutger leaned forward and kissed both of Julian's eyes tenderly. Julian had never been kissed like that before. All of Rutger's pent-up passion seemed somehow to express itself in a superior gentleness. Then he stood up, cracked his knuckles, and said, "Let's make another date, later in the week. How's that? Hey And we'll see how we feel then."

"Okay," Julian said, disengaging himself from Rutger. "Okay.

Tonight was the night he finally killed himself, Julian thought, as he stood waiting for the bus on Princess Street. His evening had gone full circle, as empty now as when it began. The bus turned the corner, he signaled the driver, it stopped. He got on, paid, found a seat mid-way back. His face looked into the clichéd urban night, the Eugene Sue dream-world of prostitutes and drug-dealing and dreams gone sour. We love cities because of their sameness, Julian thought, and hate them for it. He remembered the first time his parents took the family to New York. That was a trip. They anticipated it for months, he and Brooke and Kirsten, united in feverish excitement. They flew into JFK, stayed in a hotel on Central Park. From the United Nations to Grant's Tomb to the Metropolitan Museum of Art, they did it all. He had a photograph somewhere of the three of them holding hands on the boat to the Statue of Liberty.

When he killed himself he'd kill all his memories, good, bad and indifferent. He went, they went. No more Julian, no more any of the things he did. And how would that affect Brooke and Kirsten and the others? Would their photographs suddenly develop a missing hole? Would their memories be altered? Would his death obliterate time and space as well as his body and spirit? He closed his eyes and willed himself to die. If only he could just evaporate painlessly, just cease to be, without the effort of slashing his wrists or taking pills or hanging himself or standing in front of an intercity train.

Mightn't he hate himself enough to will it all to end?

His forehead leaned against the glass. Not only did he want to kill himself, he *needed* to kill himself. He must do it for his own good and for everyone's good. He would do a favor, put himself out of his torment and let them get on with their lives. They'd thank him. After the few social niceties were out of the way and perfunctory regrets expressed, they'd rejoice. They'd join hands, gather in a ring and dance. They wouldn't even need to worry anymore about what to buy him for Christmas, or what pointedly not to buy him in Brooke's case.

The bus stopped. Someone got on. Rutger sat suddenly beside him, flushed and breathless.

"I ran," he panted, "all the way." Julian only gaped.

"I was wrong."

"Wrong?"

"I want to make love to you and I want to do it tonight."

"Julian took hold of Rutger's hand, ignoring the people around them, the curious looks, the nods of heads. "You ran after me?" Julian said.

"Not so far," Rutger said.

"So you could take me home?"

"We need to get off the bus," Rutger said, still winded. "My car's back by UMIST." He pressed the bell, they stood up, Julian followed Rutger down the aisle to the door and then out to the street. "This way." There on the busy street full of cars, fully in the glare of lights from a hotel entrance, Rutger kissed Julian's lips. Then he said, at least with a smile, "You're not going to cry again are you?"

They dropped their jackets in the hall and held hands, eyes on one another. Rutger's free hand gently caressed Julian's face. Now that it happened, Rutger feared this thing, wondering about the rules ... or even if there were rules. Their faces came together and they kissed. For a long time that seemed sufficient. Then Julian saw that his fingers unbuttoned Rutger's shirt, he watched them work, watched Rutger's chest emerge from beneath the fabric, a fan shape of dark black hair over symmetrical muscles, and in Rutger's eyes he saw approval. Rutger took Julian's hand and placed it on his chest as he kissed him and Julian burrowed against Rutger, as if he could never get close enough to him.

"When I was about ten," Julian said, "I stayed with my grandma, she thought I wet the bed so she put rubber sheets on and gave me a lecture. Then she shut me up in this creepy old lady's room, with needlepoint and a Bela Lugosi bedroom suite. That was always my idea of loneliness, smells of roses from my grandma's garden ... those crunchy sheets. But that was nothing," he went on, "to how I've felt since George died. Like being a prisoner, you know, without even the security of knowing where you're imprisoned or why or by whom, like I was thrown in prison and forgotten. And I've been wondering if I'd ever escape that feeling of loneliness, the way people who survive trauma say they never get over it."

When he looked up, he saw Rutger watching him.

"You've been through too much," Rutger said simply, which felt like the truth.

Julian tried to say something more, but the words died in his throat. Words, he saw, yet again, had ceased to matter. He closed his eyes, so as not to look into Rutger's, and as he did so he remembered how he felt a few months back, watching the channel at Marina del Rey at night, water flowing black beneath glittering bridges, off and away, forgetful, silent. His own thoughts felt that way now. He watched the flowing of his life's river and no longer cared to probe an impenetrable mass. He kissed Rutger's neck and slowly they slid to the floor.

Rutger felt this sex with Like as an expansion, a growth, dilation of his senses, unlike anything he'd ever known. Electricity spun through him, a tingling from head to toe, losing himself to the confluence of sex and romance. They wrestled on the floor until they produced that consummating spark, and when over it felt only partly over, as they lay intertwined on the carpet. Julian's head nestled between Rutger's face and shoulder. He listened to the gentle rhythm of Rutger's breathing.

When he lifted his head he saw Rutger's eyes and the beautiful soft skin with its dark foliage of lash, his pursed mouth, satisfied expression. He said, "In here, with you, well ... I mean, out there is a world which is hard and unforgiving."

"Forget the world," Rutger told him.

"I've been worried, you know ... that I was crazy."

"Things have been changing for you, too many changes too fast like. A door slamming, a cloud passing, a haircut, they all change our world like, but we aren't crazy to be bothered ... about the way the haircut looked or that the door slamming disturbed us. Right?"

"Right."

"So change isn't madness, sometimes change is sanity."

Julian awoke from his nightmare, became slowly aware of his location, and even more slowly regained his senses. He rose stiffly, rubbing his eyes where fatigue lingered. Rutger slept soundly, hair tousled, mouth pursed, in the disarranged bed in which the two men had recently made love. Like a puppet Julian moved stiffly to the window, Like the silver-amber moon, which washed over the trees outside the window, his thoughts dissipated, drawing themselves out into thin fibers. His life passed by him then, a vision in a mirror, and if he wanted to he could have reached out and touched the moments of his own life, the life George's death had stolen from him.

Standing there he reviewed endearing childhood moments, moments which had not recurred to him for years, a hotel room in Yosemite, running through his grandparents' vineyards with his cousins, talking great plans with a school friend, his first plane flight. The images floated past cinematically, assailed him, called out, and he knew that this was his own King Lear. His own madness. He would never return to that life he left behind. He willed tears to come, to purge him of his bile of madness, but none came. He held his eyes open painfully, too long, until they ached, but the sparse moisture which begrudgingly appeared there could hardly be called a tear. Lost. Hollow. The marionette-master released his strings, and Julian's blind eyes stared heedlessly out at the silver-amber moon.

Rutger stretched in sleep, his arms extended behind his head, then he jerked once, his eyes flickered open and rested with sky-blue clarity on Julian. Then he got out of bed, went over to Julian and kissed him with the most profound and intense passion ... to which Julian responded as never he had done with another man. In that kiss he ran headlong into himself, and in that dark world of shadows and betrayal he began truly to understand himself for the first time.

Julian opened the front door of Kirsten and Alec's and come into the lobby brimming with something new and different, something he wanted desperately to share with Kirsten. But he stopped short when he saw her at her laptop, which sat on her lovely old mahogany desk. He knew something was terribly wrong.

"Kirsten?"

She turned to him with eyes brimful with tears. "It's an email from mom," she said. Then, taking a breath, "She says that Brooke destroyed your apartment ... furniture, pictures, manuscripts, electronics ... well, Like ... everything."

He stood and stared at her.

"So," Kirsten said, "Mom says there's honestly not much that's salvageable. I guess Chris hurled an enormous amount into the pool, and they're asking that you pay for the damage. Mom and Dad will do that, of course ... no problem."

Julian still stood staring at her, unable to express a single word.

"So. Mom wants to know if you'd like them to call the police. It is a crime, Julian. And besides that, it's simply unconscionable, to ... " She fought back tears. "To basically obliterate someone's home."

He sat hard on the sofa.

"Do you need time to think?"

He looked at her. "No. Don't call the police. But would you ask mom to convey a message to Brooke for me."

"Okay."

"Turn and let me see you writing it," Julian said.

Kirsten did as she was told.

His voice choking now with emotion, Like told her to write, "Tell mom to ask Chris if it brought George back from the dead. If it did ... then would you ask her to tell George how much I love him and how much I've missed him. But if it didn't, would you tell her that I shall never forgive her, not if we should both live into our 100s."

Kirsten had been typing away as he spoke. She concluded and turned to him.

"Hit send, but copy me on it ... I want to see what you said."

She put him into the copy line and hit send.

Picking up the postcard her mother had left lying on the mantle, a stunned Brooke saw a photograph of the Manchester skyline. Not for an instant could she understand why her mother would leave the vile thing out, as if a card had been sent her from a normal person on a normal holiday. This shitty missive should have been tossed straight in the trash. So Brooke tore it in half, tore the halves in two and then, when she could tear it no more and simply struggled against the elementary laws of physics, she angrily threw the offending pieces into the fireplace. Leaning back against the mantle, catching her breath and closing her eyes once again to the pain, she remembered something. She remembered the car accident they saw the day before George's death.

"An accident," George said solemnly. But behind his dutiful solemnity, Brooke caught a five year old's enthusiasm for the macabre.

"I don't like him seeing this," she said.

"What can I do?" Wyatt shot back.

"George," she said, "George, sit down."

"But I want to see."

"I didn't ask you whether you wanted to see or not. I said to sit down. Now. And put your seatbelt back on. I mean it, young man."

Wyatt came to a stop behind the car in front of him. Traffic struggled, restricted to one lane, red lights flashed, policemen stood manfully in the road. An ambulance had parked across the median, a car sat up on the sidewalk, someone lay in the road. One of the policemen looked in at them as they passed by, in his eyes she saw their reflection, saw a white middle-class family in their Volvo station wagon, insulated from tragedy, safe from misfortune. But she knew that was untrue, and she wished she could find that young policeman and tell him about George's death the very next day. No one was safe from misfortune, she thought now.

"Someone's been hit," she said softly.

"I think maybe it's a dog," Wyatt said.

"No," she said, even softer, "of course it's not a dog."

"I want to see," George said.

"Sit still," she said, the strain of her attempted distraction evident in her voice, "You can wear your green swimsuit tomorrow."

She felt Wyatt's quick look at her, an awareness of her worry.

"It's not a green swimsuit," George said, "it's a Ninja Turtle suit."

"The color is green," she said.

"Yeah," he agreed, then said logically, "but it's got Ninjas on it."

"Well, you can wear the green Ninja Turtle suit then," she said. "You can tell Uncle Julian you're a Ninja."

"I'm not a Ninja. I just have a Ninja Turtle suit."

Brooke looked out her window and saw the medics and the elderly woman, who must have been thrown a great distance. Probably she'd been in the crosswalk farther down the road. It seemed as if her leg were missing. Perhaps it merely bent them underneath her? She turned back to George, who strained to see out the window. Her hand ruffled his blond head. "I love you, honey."

"Will Uncle Julian have a Ninja suit do you think?"

"I doubt it."

"Why not?"

"I don't think Uncle Julian wears Ninja swimsuits."

"Can I call him when I get home?"

"Yes. But you have to promise to talk to grandma too. It's rude to call there and not talk to grandma. Do you understand? You'll hurt grandma's feelings and you don't want to do that."

"I always talk to grandma."

"That's good then," she said. She looked at Wyatt, who tried too hard not to look at the dead woman. He no longer thought it was a dog.

Suddenly traffic opened up. They were past the accident. Wyatt headed for the San Diego Freeway, turning up the radio on the oldies station he favored. Sometimes he and George sang along to the songs they both recognized. George had a good memory for songs.

"I'm going to bring you back a seashell, daddy," George said, "because I will be looking for seashells tomorrow."

"I don't know if there are any seashells on that particular beach," Wyatt said.

"But I want to find one."

"Well," Wyatt laughed, "you can't find, sport, if one isn't there."

"Mama, daddy's teasing me," George said.

"He's not teasing you. He's telling you that there may not be any seashells on that beach.

After a moment's silence George asked, "how many shopping days until Christmas, mama?"

She and Wyatt both laughed, then she reached back again and rubbed George's hair.

Brooke stared down at the pieces of postcard. George went looking for seashells, didn't he, to bring home to Wyatt? That's why he wandered away from Julian. She closed her eyes. It would be a cold day in hell before she told Julian that information; it would be a cold day in hell before she told anyone that information.

10

After a wonderful and romantic lunch with Rutger, in which they someone managed to drink a bottle of *Pinot Noir*, eat spaghetti Bolognese, hold hands and kiss – all at the same time – Julian walked the city center. He didn't feel like taking the bus today, and from the city center he certainly could find a taxi to Didsbury. At his last birthday party, George had been so cute. 'With my balloons,' he kept repeating to his father, who held a video phone in his hand, 'with my balloons.' Julian told him that they could play some video games later. George ran in circles around the back lawn with the girl from next door. When he got in trouble for dragging his cat across the patio by its tail he sulked and nearly cried and said, in the non sequitur fashion of children, 'I don't want my balloons any more, daddy.'

Always George's favorite uncle, Julian found George special to him as well, with his prescient blue eyes, his scuffed shoes, his precocious way of talking. They played Legos, Julian helped him build the house pictured on the front of the box but which demanded coordination beyond George's capacities. George carried the house around with him saying, 'Uncle Julian made me my house.' 'That's nice,' his grandmother said, 'now come and play outside with the others.' Something at the same time liberated and horrified Julian in this thinking about George as a real person.

A black taxi pulled alongside, the driver looked at Julian and Julian looked at the driver, then he opened the door and climbed into the backseat.

"Where to?" the driver asked.

"Didsbury."

"The village?"

"Yes, just off Fog Lane," Julian said, and he recalled his last real conversation with Brooke, early on the day of the accident.

They sat over lemonade on their parent's patio, because they'd escaped the family members gathered for the annual family reunion.

"Here you two are," Aunt Meredith said, coming around the edge of the cabana. "We've been looking everywhere for you."

"Hi," Julian said.

"Have Wyatt and George arrived yet?" Brooke asked.

"Hi and yes. Wyatt's playing scrabble with Judy and Louise. Your mom's talking on the phone, George's sitting on her lap."

Julian looked at her and then he looked at Brooke, "Aunt Meredith, do you know I'm gay?"

Brooke's eyes went wide.

He wasn't sure why he asked it. But he did.

Aunt Meredith held her palms up. "Everybody says so. I guess I knew."

"Does it bother you?" he asked.

"Bother?"

"Do you disapprove?"

"Why? Are you doing it on purpose to bother people?"

"Of course not," he said.

"Exactly. And I didn't know I was entitled to an opinion," Meredith said,

"I figured it bothered you."

"How come? Did I say something?" she asked.

"No. Not exactly."

She sat on the wall and looked at the two of them. "Just how come you asked me that?"

"We've been talking."

"People think you don't want us here," Meredith said to Julian.

"He doesn't," Brooke said.

Julian felt himself color. "Only because I thought you disapproved of me."

"Everybody's proud of you," Meredith said, "on account of you're so intelligent and talk so well."

"Brooke shouldn't have said that."

"Why not?" Brooke said. "Let's be truthful around here for once."

"Truth isn't something you want to toss around unnecessarily, dear," Aunt Meredith said. "It can damn well tear families apart, the truth can."

Brooke wrinkled her brow at this pretend profundity. "So we should lie?"

"Sometimes, and we should respect everyone's needs and everyone's secrets and everyone's vulnerable soft spots. You don't hear me asking why you look like Ricky Raccoon and asking questions about you and Wyatt? Do you?"

"What would you ask?" Brooke said. Her hands rubbed her eyes, but it didn't help.

"I wouldn't ask anything," Aunt Meredith said. "I thought I made that clear."

Brooke looked at Julian.

Meredith gestured upward. "God I love winter. Don't get skies like that in the summer."

"How's your arthritis?" Julian asked.

She shrugged.

Brooke stood up. "This ... whatever it is ... is giving me a headache."

"Why?"

Meredith ignored them. "Trouble with these family reunion things is that they don't mean a damn thing. They're just a gimmick."

"A gimmick?" Julian said.

149

"Nothing to it. They're garbage. Look at you two gossiping and going after me. What kind of dinner are we going to have? You don't want us here, and I'd rather be home with Admiral – he's that new two-tone weiner dog your Uncle Alvin gave me – fixing our dinner." She looked at Brooke and shrugged, deferring pointedly to her lower social rank with the comment, "Some pepper steak and muffins, to be exact. I make them from this mix I get at Costco, they're really good. Ask your mother." Then she looked again at Brooke and inclined her head toward Julian. "I'm pretty sure mister slim-figure there won't be eating muffins, mix or scratch."

Brooke smiled at that. Then she shrugged.

"You go ahead and be gay if you want," she said to Julian, "and you go ahead and stay in your unhappy marriage," she said with mischievousness to Brooke. "Me? I'm going to go watch the scrabble game and sneak some more of your mom's almond bark." And then, disingenuously she asked them, "How's she make it anyway? That stuff's good."

She stood up and put a hand momentarily on their arms, as if she were pretending to be a priest after church on Sunday. Then she left.

"Well, I'll be goddamned," Julian said. He tilted his head back and looked up into the sky.

Brooke brushed her hair back, her mouth opened as if she were going to say something. She twiddled her fingers, then her mouth shut. It grew still. " Don't forget, you're taking George to the beach before dinner. You promised him." Then, bitterly, "Scrabble in the meantime, you kiss-up?"

An hour and a half later, Julian left for the beach with George.

He looked at the back of the taxi driver's head, perfectly framed against the advancing glass front of the Cooperative Insurance Building, and he thought this:

Brooke didn't like him before he let her son drown. Maybe Brooke never really liked him. And then he thought, 'Maybe I never liked her either.'

"Stop here please," he told the taxi driver.

"This is still the city center, mate. You've got four miles out to Didsbury."

"I know. But let me out here."

He paid the fare, climbed out, and with no destination in mind started walking.

Brooke wandered around the women's department for the better part of an hour. Though she fingered a number of garments, she had yet to try anything on. She thought she traced the pattern of a figure-eight on the floor. Some salesperson would notice that, she'd better buy something. So without thinking further she grabbed a skirt and a blouse and walked straightaway into one of the dressing rooms, where she took off her dress and tried them on.

The blouse was several sizes too big, while the skirt proved practically unzippable it was so tight. She looked like a clown. She ripped them off and tossed them furiously on the floor, then she unhooked her bra and closely examined her breasts in the three-sided mirror. Seen like this they were still rather nice. Wyatt was right. They had an excellent color and were firm. A gentle suckler, George never bit her and he didn't pull hard. She smiled to herself, thinking that she might just walk off through the mall like this, displaying her great tits. Why not? Nothing to be ashamed of in having a good set of hooters, she thought.

But she dressed again and picked up the clothes from the floor. Forgetting completely that they didn't fit, and that she hadn't wanted them in the first place, she took them to the saleslady. With only a moment's hesitation, the slightest trembling of her hand over the computer-scanner gun, the saleslady betrayed her knowledge that these were the wrong clothes. Clearly she felt torn over saying something. However, she merely scanned the tickets and rang up the sale, announcing the price and then taking Brooke's card from her hand and running that through a scanning machine as well. A purchase agreement spilled forth with little rachety noises, and with a pen the saleslady handed it across the counter.

Brooke signed for her expensive and unwanted merchandise.

"Thank you, Mrs. Eiffel," the saleslady said.

Brooke started.

"Brooke," she said tartly.

"What?"

"My name."

"*What*?" the saleslady asked, visibly confused.

"My name is Brooke, it is not Mrs. anything."

"Well, honey ... I don't care," the saleslady said politely, "I mean it's okay with me, but it doesn't say Brooke on your card, does it? So how could I know? But if you go up to credit they can change it, then you can have them --"

"Oh, for crying out loud," Brooke snorted, "just give me the goddamned mini-skirt."

The saleslady handed the bag over, her mouth open as if again she might depart from procedure and say something, perhaps 'Thanks, Brooke,' though she didn't. She remained silent. Brooke ran toward the escalator and, in her haste, nearly overturned a spinning rack of tank-tops and denim shorts. She stopped a moment, stared at the wildly spinning shorts and swaying tank-tops, composed herself, and then walked slowly toward the escalator. Call her what she would, Brooke thought, she had a better pair of tits than the chubby little saleslady would ever even dream about.

He stood outside the steps to The Royal Exchange and faced empty St. Anne's Square. A car back-fired, too close, and he all but leapt into a shop window. The glass quivered menacingly, he felt the shock waves against his head. He simply stood there in front of the shimmering glass. The adrenaline rush of alarm receded only slowly. The glass ceased reverberating, the sidewalk grew quiet. Rutger looked around him a moment, observing any observers. Then he banged his head back hard against the window. It quivered again, but his adrenaline had ebbed away.

He liked St. Anne's Square, it made Manchester seem beautiful. Lights glittered in the windows of the flats above the shops. In one room he saw a TV flicker, in another a shirt less man cut his nails. He thought about Julian, thought about Julian's handsome face, about the deep dimples when he smiled, he even thought about the way Julian moved his hands. Rutger's head strained upward. A marquee of stars threw themselves over the sky, he felt sucked up into them, they seemed to emit noise as well as light, as if he touched them as well as looked at them.

He walked the remaining blocks, until he looked down the stairwell into the club where Annabella's sister, whom he awakened with a phone call, said he would find her. But he saw no Annabella, only bodies and smoke amid the music. After a moment's hesitation he swept down into the melee, pushed his way toward the bar, fought for attention, ordered a pint of lager, and then clawed his way to a resting point beside a pillar. From there he watched the young, nicely dressed, well-to-do crowd, listened to the music, sipped his beer.

A bra-less young woman in orange and purple kissed a man with a bluish pallor. Smoke funneled through his nose as they kissed, residual from the cigarette which hung erect from his fingers. A disoriented tourist in a suit had shed his tie, which stuck out from a bulging jacket pocket. He gyrated to the music, back and forth on his feet, watery eyes searching the crowd like radar. The song pounded from speakers, butchered into near unrecognizability by the lack of treble. The tourist seemed to know the words, however, he mouthed them to himself as he bounced from foot to foot.

"*Rutger?*"

"Annabella."

Done up smartly, her lips glowed with maroon lipstick, her arms and fingers bangled and ringed. She kissed him softly on each cheek, then she took his beer from his hand and, as she sipped it, said pointedly, "I never knew you came here."

"I don't. I came to find you," he said.

She thought about that a moment. "Why?"

"Because I'm in love – and it makes me think about things ... important thing."

Somehow his answer seemed to irritate her, almost as if his being there forced issues to the surface that she thought better left on the lake bottom. But she asked him, "What things?"

"All sorts."

She put a hand in the middle of his back. "You'd better explain to me."

"You remember the American from that day in Didsbury? The one I told you showed up in Bolton?"

"Mostly," she said. "I remember you telling me he came into the shop in Bolton."

"I met him again last week, at a gay pub," and he gestured the several blocks toward the gay village. "I was there, he was there, we got along well. He wanted to come home with me, I put him off, then I finally decided that I wanted him to come home with me, so I chased after his bus, got on, found him, kissed him on the lips there on Whitworth Street, made him come back with me ..." his voice fell away and he was silent.

"And?" she asked.

"And he's the love of my life, I think," Rutger said, "And he's head-over-heels for me too, I can tell. But I didn't think about what it might do to him, mean to him I suppose I mean. It's hard to explain. Life after death."

"*Life after death*?" Annabella stared into Rutger's beer, which she still held in her hand, as if she saw through something. She felt lightheaded, tired, out of her league. "Rutger, why've you come looking for me like this in the middle of the night?"

Annabella had never before spoken to him in that tone of voice; it arrested him. For too long a time for it to be accidental they remained silent.

"I needed to talk with you," Rutger said at last, "so I rang you, your sister said I'd find you here. Do you mind terribly, then?"

She considered carefully what she ought to say, but looking into his eyes she found herself unable to articulate her real thoughts. "No, you know I don't mind. But maybe it's this American you should go find, not me."

"Julian," Rutger said, "his name's Julian."

"Maybe you should go find Julian."

"I saw him earlier this evening, and we made smashing sex. But, yes," he said thoughtfully. Then he met her eyes. "Maybe I should."

She leaned forward, put her arms around him and buried her lips in his neck. "You're on your own in this one. You know I can't guide you, don't you?"

"I'm not asking you to guide me," he said.

"But you are."

He said below his closed eyes, "I love you, Annabella."

"And I love you too, Rutger."

He shrugged, taking back his beer from her. They stood silently, side by side, watching the tourist and the bra-less woman.

She took his hand. "Dance with me?"

"All right."

They made their way more or less into the middle of the room, which seemed to constitute the dance floor. A new song played now over the speakers and they moved along with the throng. Periodically Annabella smiled up at him sweatily, a smile with which Rutger had grown familiar. They stopped their shaking and moved back to the place by the pillar. Rutger gulped down the little bit of the beer.

"You dance good like, for a Lancashire lad," Annabella said.

"Thanks."

"But gay men always do, don't they?"

He laughed and she smiled at him. The music surged around them.

"Something more to drink, then?" he asked her.

She hesitated a moment then said, "Grapefruit and soda."

He moved toward the bar, pushed through the human barrier, ordered, paid, and then managed to work his way back to Annabella and the safety of their pillar. "Cheers."

"Cheers." She lifted the glass to her lips and gestured toward a pretty girl. "You're being watched, you are."

"Always."

"She's deciding if you're taken."

"So am I," he said.

"You know how to be witty, you do, Rutger Whitaker." Her head inclined toward the rear of the disco. "There's a patio, not so crowded. We might even be able to sit."

"All right, then."

She took them across the dance floor, through coils of arms and legs, into a place of even sharper music. They passed through that purgatory, through an archway, and emerged into an enclosed brick courtyard, where fairy lights were strung overhead. It wasn't quiet, it wasn't particularly private, and it was certainly cold, but it was an improvement. They sat side by side on a bench. Rutger leaned his head back and looked up into the sky. Clouds slowly gathered, he imagined he heard thunder, imagined that the flickers of fairy lights were lightening. They sipped their drinks.

"What thing do you most regret in your life?" she asked.

"One thing?"

"Thing you regret most."

"Why?"

"It tells you a bucket about someone, doesn't it?" she said.

He looked at her from the corner of his eyes, measuring her interest. 'That I waited so long to come out ... that I waited so long to find someone like Julian."

She took a cigarette from a packet in her purse, lit it, and inhaled powerfully. " You want me to be honest, then, our Rutger?"

"Aren't you always?"

"No," she said and she looked at him boldly. "I knew that you lived in the past but if you'd said you regretted something to do with self-improvement, or, I don't know, something of that sort, I wouldn't have thought it then. But what you say, about this man, it tells me you've moved on ... you've broken down the frigging Berlin Wall."

He shut his eyes and leaned his head back against the wall. Noises closed in around him. What she said about him, couldn't it just as easily be said about Julian? Didn't he live in the past too? Another couple came outside, he heard them speaking softly.

He opened his eyes. "Dance with me again, Annabella. Please?"

An old song pounded, the singer crooned, the bass hammered, colored lights swirled. Sweat dribbled down Rutger's brow into his eyes, his shirt clung to him, from his chest rose a faint odor of long-dead cologne. One finger of one hand crooked lazily through one of Annabella's fingers and they danced without looking at one another. But then their eyes met suddenly and he smiled, rubbing sweat off his forehead and mouthing, 'enough?'

She nodded.

They hurried up the staircase and outside. The street seemed quiet after the chaos of the disco. They walked slowly down toward the gay village. In the moonlight a wisp-drifting pale mist rose from the surface of the canal, the promenade deserted. Beneath a streetlight he looked at her, as she lit another cigarette and smoked it passionlessly. Her feet clomped loudly on the paving stones as they crossed slumbering Princess Street and walked down to the canal's edge. A block of newly converted flats loomed inauspiciously on the horizon. They stood and looked at the water.

When he glanced sideways at her, she smoked with her eyes closed, oblivious to him. Moonlight dribbled over her, she smelled of patchouli. She opened her eyes and they were as hollow, as sunken as Julian's when he appeared that day in Bolton, ringed by fatigued white splotches. He faintly heard a car pass on an adjoining street. Water gurgled, and Rutger put a hand over his eyes a moment and listened to the water.

He had looked up a photo on his phone tonight for Julian, of the annual company picnic last summer in Heaton Park. Rutger felt attached to Heaton Park, he practically grew up on its footpaths. In the photo, Annabella posed by the very food tables where Rutger's father had his last picnic with his family. In the photograph, summery and sultry Annabella had her hands on her head, holding hot hair from her face, beneath her tan all smiles. A bit drunk on the edge of the canal, Rutger could not shake that photograph from his mind.

"What's it you're thinking about?" she asked him.

"You," he said.

She shook her head at him and closed her eyes. "I'm going back," she said sadly, and he understood the source of that sadness. "It's chilly."

"Need me to walk you?"

"No, of course not." She tossed her cigarette in a calculated arc into the canal. "Where's this Julian gone home to after your smashing sex, then? Home to Didsbury?"

"I don't know." And in his tone of voice, his look, the very sound of his words he knew that he gave away everything, every feeling, every nuance of desire. "Probably."

She kissed him on his neck, held his arm a moment, "You're changing before my eyes."

"I'm not."

"You are and I want you to. It's good, Rutger, it is. You have to change to ..." her voice fell away and she shrugged and waved her hand as if it were a wand. "Screw them all, the wankers."

"Who?"

"Them. The world. The Geralds and the Pamelas and others. Screw them all."

"All right," he agreed, "screw them all."

She kissed him again, then scuttled up the stairs to Princess Street. He watched her disappear into side street murk, and he knew that the Annabella who'd been as close as a girlfriend to him had gone forever.

II

Rutger sat on the wall and the canal's putrid smell filled up his head. Water lapped below him, a Great Gatsby light blinked a few hundred yards down the promenade. Rutger stared at it, losing himself in the stars and darkness. Although an occasional car passed by the road behind him, it was almost noiseless, just a misty-foggy hush. He turned his head again toward the blinking light, which seemed the only significant contact he had just then with the world of other people. A sudden splash in the water brought his look downward. The surface of the water had an oily glint but he thought he just caught some movement. A fish? In this polluted canal? Refracted twists and turns seemed to bubble up from the water. A fish, he felt sure of it, and he felt more than observed its departure out toward the locks.

Julian's hand fell on his back and Rutger started. Their eyes met. For a moment they merely looked at one another, then Julian climbed up on the wall and sat beside Rutger.

"I thought I might find you here."

"Great minds thinking alike, then," Rutger said.

"I missed you," Julian told him, "I'm thinking maybe it's what you call love."

Rutger thought about that and looked quizzically at Julian. "Do you love me?"

"I don't know. Yes, probably. You know what I mean."

"It's okay between us," Rutger said, "isn't it?"

"I hope so," Julian told him.

Rutger's eyes gently closed a moment. Julian thought it a lovely gesture. Then Rutger shrugged, "I love you, Julian, my American."

Julian said nothing, but he nodded his head. Then he pulled Rutger to him, and put his arm around his waist. Rutger's head quite naturally leaned against Julian's shoulder and his own arm drifted out and around Julian's waist. Still they said nothing. The light continued to blink, the misty-foggy canal shrouded them, nothing seemed to move in the city behind them. Rutger breathed in Julian's clean American soapy smell, the rough texture of Julian's sweater scratched his cheek, his own hand tucked up to the knuckles inside Julian's trouser pocket. When he looked up, out of the corner of his eye, he saw that Julian tossed him a similar look. Though they laughed, still it stayed quiet between them.

Rutger broke the silence. "I told my best friend Annabella about you, and she's made me see tonight that it means, really means ... as Robert Graves said, 'goodbye to all that.'"

"Goodbye to what?" Julian wondered.

"All that pretending, all that trying to be what you're meant to be in this country, all the lies. All that."

"I'm scared," Julian said, which wasn't at all what he intended to say, which wasn't even what he thought. But those are the words he said.

"I know."

Their faces came close together, nearly touching. Rutger lifted Julian's chin and kissed his mouth, his taste salty, real, Rutger had never tasted a mouth so real. Julian's tongue rolled over Rutger's teeth as if counting them, then it found Rutger's tongue, prodded it, lay hard upon it. Rutger heard himself sigh, gentle sighing, far-off sighing, like the blinking light, the canal. They pulled back from their kiss and embraced. Rutger heard that splash again, but this time he didn't look down, nor did he look at the blinking light, nor at Manchester nor at anything else. He looked at Julian.

It began to feel cold, so they climbed down from the wall and Rutger drew Julian's arm around him. Eerily bright, the sky blossomed with stars. Julian gestured that he wished to walk, and they went down the promenade, and turned up into the dimly lit red-light district near the railway station. Their breath drifted back over their heads, their feet crunched on the paving stones, the moon hung low and worthless overhead. They were quiet, as if words might only push them apart, and it seemed like they walked for miles. At the end of a lane between warehouses and the rump of the Rochdale Canal, they reached a 'T' junction, where they looked down on the lights of Piccadilly station.

Still silent they returned along the lane, but half-way back stopped again to kiss, and Rutger's hands slipped beneath Julian's shirt and he found his lover's flesh. With Julian's texture beneath his fingers, Julian's smell at his nose, the stars, the alien sense of time and place, Rutger felt dizzy. His lips just touched against Julian's and they breathed together a moment. Then he gathered Julian to him, afraid and yet completely determined, lost and angry, eager, touched by profundity and banality at the very same time. His eyes closed and they kissed.

"I think I could come to love you forever, then, Julian," Rutger said.

"Yes," Julian agreed, "I think you could."

In the aftermath of sex they tumbled together in Rutger's bed, the duvet crushed back to the foot, exhausted by their recent passion. Rutger's hand lay in the middle of Julian's chest. He leaned up on his elbow. Even in the room's indistinct greenish-blue glimmer he found Julian perfectly visible to him, felt him smile up from the pillow as his hand slid gently down Rutger's back. Rutger brought his head down and kissed Julian's chest, drifted kisses down to his stomach.

"You didn't kill him," he whispered.

"You weren't there," Julian said.

"But I know you, Julian, and so I know what happened."

"You don't know." Julian pulled himself up beside Rutger and murmured in his ear, "but thank you."

"You didn't kill him," Rutger echoed, putting his mouth next to Julian's head and saying his own words as quietly as breath itself. "We're good together."

"Yes."

Rutger waited for the 'I love you' which never came. So he asked, "Can we say this is the start of something real, then?"

Julian looked at Rutger a moment, then he closed his eyes, "Yes ... because it is. Lying here right now," Julian told him, "I feel stronger than I've felt in months. I feel better. I think I'm going straight out to Didsbury, I think I'm going to pack my bags, and go ... somewhere. I don't know where." He concentrated, and in concentrating he thought of loose ends which needed tidying up. "I know I can't stay any longer with Kirsten. No," he corrected himself, "I know I don't want to stay any longer with Alec and Kirsten."

"And us?" Rutger asked.

"Stay with me?" Julian said and his words hung fire.

Then Julian curled closer to Rutger and silently kissed his neck. "Now, I'm off to Didsbury and ... it might take me more than a day or two to tidy things up with my sister, but then ..."

Brooke remembered thinking that Father Shoemaker held out his arms theatrically, a little too aware of symbol, myth and ritual. She recalled him spread-eagled against a blue winter sky, a 'Christ-on-the-cross' motif. But, as he spoke, he looked them in the face and despite her skepticism Brooke felt reassured. The performance contained magic, and not the magic of a mountebank but a white-light magic which signified, which connected loose ends. After all, as their cultural safe place, the Episcopal Church took them from childhood to adulthood. Perhaps it even expressed something of George himself, or whatever George had become. What did Episcopalians believe of the afterlife anyway? Not much. George as a semi-cognizant bolt of light? Brooke visualized the afterlife that way, when she studied for confirmation. Maybe, in the end, all the mumbo jumbo only meant something to a grieving mother. Brooke , after all, had requested beautiful Rite One.

In the midst of life we are in death;
from whom can we seek help?
From you alone, O lord,
who by our sins are justly angered.
Holy God, Holy and Mighty,
Holy and merciful Savior,
deliver us not into the bitterness of eternal
death.

Lord, you know the secrets of our hearts;
shut not your ears to our prayers,
but spare us, O Lord.

Holy God, Holy and Mighty,
Holy and merciful Savior,
deliver us not into the bitterness of eternal
death.

O wórthy and eternal Judge,
do not let the pains of death
turn us away from you at our last hour.

Holy God, Holy and Mighty,
Holy and merciful Savior,
deliver us not into the bitterness of eternal
death.

Wyatt and several other relatives tossed a
handful of earth on the coffin. There were some
protracted noiseless moments, when no one seemed
able to look at anyone else, an intimidating

maladroitness pinioning them. They clearly didn't know what to make of this last brooding over little George's boxed-up cadaver.

"In sure and certain hope of the resurrection to eternal life through our Lord Jesus Christ, we commend to Almighty God our brother George, and we commit his body to the ground; earth to earth, ashes to ashes, dust to dust. The Lord bless him and keep him, the Lord make his face to shine upon him and be gracious to him, the Lord lift up his countenance upon him and give him peace. Amen."

Only then did Brooke dare sneak a glance at Julian, whose red eyes were puffy. Cradled beneath a thoughtful friend's arm – some overdressed faggot in a Ralph Lauren sport coat and boots with metal buckles -- he stood boldly there in front of everyone. As Brooke watched, the friend gently kissed Julian's neck and Julian nuzzled him back. Then Julian had seen Brooke watching them and tried to smile. Brooke remembered how curtly she turned away, and how desperately she sought out her own meager safety in Wyatt's embrace.

"The God of peace, who brought again from the dead our Lord Jesus Christ, the great shepherd of the sheep, through the blood of the everlasting covenant: Make you perfect in every good work to do his will, working in you that which is well-pleasing in his sight; through Jesus Christ, to whom be glory for ever and ever. Amen."

Thinking about Father Shoemaker at George's funeral caused Brooke to remember an experience she had with Julian. The summer Kirsten went back East to a camp on Cape Cod, Brooke and Julian were left alone with the parents, Julian, overcome by a sort of holy sense of his gayness, decided that being gay didn't mean he had to turn away from the church.

Usually Brooke and Kirsten ignored him on the subject of religion, but in those days after Kirsten departed for New York, Julian regaled Brooke with the possibilities for spirituality, the need for reconciliation, the fact that Christ's love could embrace them all, gay and straight. And then, inevitably, given his receptiveness, he got wind of a gay Episcopalian group, which met at St. Cuthbert's, their own church. For five expectant days he discussed the group and begged Brooke to go with him for a meeting and, bored as she'd been that summer, any adventure seemed adventure enough, so she went.

On the way to church, in the car, Julian sweated buckets. He turned the air-conditioning vents full on his face. Brooke had never seen him so hopeful. Somehow this seemed to authenticate everything. They parked and Julian popped breath mints into his mouth, because his knowledge that he would meet the men of his fantasies, men at once handsome, successful, brave and Episcopalian lurked unspoken between them. He combed his hair twice in the rearview mirror, and then he put his hand on Brooke's shoulder and said, "I'm so glad you can share this with me, Chrissie. You've no idea what it means to me."

Complimented, Brooke nonetheless found his intensity off-putting. Actually, she thought he'd never been more handsome, his eyes shining, in his button-down cotton shirt, his chinos, his penny loafers. At the very least he looked like the man of his dreams. But the moment they stepped through the door into the side chapel Brooke saw the expression on Julian's face. His eyes drained of light, his face almost seemed to pale. A Saint on the cross must have looked like that. And Brooke, who had a more acute vision for being uninvolved, looked out into the chapel and saw what her brother saw: an armada of misfits.

They wore too-tight jeans and muscle-displaying 'T' shirts, most of which they'd tucked into the too-tight jeans. Mostly there were cowboy boots on their feet rather than penny loafers. Not only did no dashingly handsome men come into sight, no one Brooke or Julian would have called a normal Episcopalian appeared, certainly no one successful or brave or dreamy. They seemed a needy crew, as they turned vampire eyes on the well-dressed interlopers from that other Episcopalian world from which they'd long ago fled into this subterranean existence. Julian slumped into a pew and Brooke, nearly giddy now, slumped beside him. The worst, however, was yet to come.

The priest, who no doubt meant well, invited them to come forward and gather in a semi-circle around the altar, where he started the host around the line with the wine following after. The host, though, seemed unlike anything Brooke and Julian had *ever* seen, a slab of glutinous homemade wheat bread. Each communicant tore off a bit and handed it to the next person, saying "body of Christ, the bread of heaven," as he did so.

To Julian's right stood a man no taller than five feet five, stick thin, reeking of cigarettes. Nervous at Julian's presence, he tore off an enormous chunk of bread and handed it to Julian who, dutiful Episcopalian, plopped it straightaway into his mouth. He nearly choked. His eyes bulged, he gasped, he turned quickly to Brooke, and managed only to mumble something like 'wawee uhf wife' before offering her in his turn an appropriately minuscule shard of the foul organic bread. Even now, years after the fiasco, Brooke found it hard to contain her laughter.

Poor Julian. How cruelly his dreams were destroyed. They'd driven home in stupefied silence and once there Julian threw himself on his bed, face to the wall, crying his eyes out. Pathetic. Their mother, who of course had no inkling of the nature of the problem, and couldn't be brought fully into the picture, made him a glass of lemonade and sat beside him, stroking his arm and telling him that things would feel better soon. Who knew what she thought was wrong? Brooke floated on a raft in the pool and laughed so wildly that she gulped water when she tumbled off while still laughing. Nothing in all her life had seemed so funny. Only later -- with deeper reflection -- did the true slap of the experience come home to her, and did the significance of the moment make itself real.

Now, Julian laughed too when reminded of the event. But he suffered. Reflecting, Brooke's mood changed suddenly and her mirth disappeared. Good, she thought. Excellent, in fact. Let him suffer, the asshole. She turned off the living room light -- she sat by herself in the middle of her three-seater Laura Ashley sofa -- and then slowly she got up, climbed the stairs, undressed, and slithered into bed beside Wyatt.

In the restroom, Julian closed his eyes a moment and wondered at the hidden message in the birdsong that came through an open window. Leaving the restroom he walked down a flight of steps, then went out to a garden arbor, where shade gathered peacefully. He lay his head on his arm and thought about Rutger, George, his life, though mostly Rutger – with whom he was taking a day trip to the country.

One memory still haunted him. In Kindergarten, a boy locked himself in the bathroom and refused to come out. What sort of 1950's prude put locking doors on kindergarten stalls anyway? Actually, the bathroom consisted only of two side-by-side stalls in the far L-shaped nook of the classroom. Students had locked themselves in the stalls before, that wasn't unusual, and most of the miscreants came out after a few minutes of cajoling, with dirty underwear or wet trousers, full of excuses. This time, the teacher's wheedles proved insufficient. She asked Julian to shimmy beneath the door and he did, where he found the boy on the other side in tears.

He didn't have messed pants, he wasn't wet, he just seemed miserable. So Julian hugged him, and held him while he sobbed. Julian never learned what the other boy cried about. Perhaps it didn't matter. After all, Julian only imitated his mother, who held him that way when he fell from the swing-set and scraped his knee. However, much later, when they were eighteen, the boy -- now a young man -- unexpectedly stopped one afternoon in the school locker room and talked to Julian. They were both in green gym shorts, shirtless, ready for the showers. Julian remembered the young man's unfashionable swept back hair, his drugged eyes vacant yet luminous, his social inferiority to the popular Julian all too apparent. They ran in contrary social circles, and that counted for much in high school.

But he stayed, they actually talked. At that point they'd had nothing to do with one another for years, they were barely even acquaintances. Yet the young man talked at length about his new motorcycle, which he called a 'chopper,' and Julian at first thought he claimed to own a helicopter, but they clarified the point. That night he drove his chopper into a palm tree and killed himself. The police adamantly declared it a suicide, they knew these things. Palm trees, barely three feet wide, weren't hit by a motorcycle unless the driver tried. Had the boy come to say good-bye to Julian, to someone who'd been nice to him those many years before? Julian never stopped wondering.

He wondered about it again today, in the garden off the Wilmslow Road.

He heard footsteps and looked up to see Rutger come down the steps to him. He sat beside him.

"I really am sorry for your suffering," Rutger said.. But I've seen a lot in life, and in the end it's this simple: Forget, forgive, let go, move on. Forget your sense of injustice, forgive yourself, let go of the pain, move on from there. You must do it, Julian."

"I know that." He leaned back on both elbows, and lifted his face to the sun. A noticeable change crept into his voice when he spoke, his words more sonorous. "The thing is ... I can't stop thinking about that ... well, that day."

"That's precisely the thing you must let go of."

"But how?"

Rutger looked him square in the face. "I don't know. That you must decipher for yourself. Do you know Ovid?"

"The Latin poet?"

"Yes. *Finis coronat opus?* The end crowns the work? We'll have to remember that, Julian."

But Julian thought instead of a song by Morrissey, not a poem by Ovid, and he told Rutger, "Come, Armageddon."

The hurt of George's death had never been more crushing. She leapt from bed and turned on the light, as if the Los Angeles Department of Water and Power could nullify those memories. It could not. They stayed, ghost-riders from a past she'd never escape. George had died and nothing would change that. She trembled beneath the image of the water, the waves, the hopeless relays of police divers -- one of whom reminded her of their cousin Laura, who went to Harvard. Every time she saw Laura now she pictured him diving for George's body.

She looked directly into the light but found no comfort in its pale warmth. Memories of other peoples' deaths come and went, but George's did not, George's only stayed and growed, and wrenched her ever closer to her own grave. She got up and sat on the chair beside the bed, dizzy with pain. Even as she closed her eyes and tilted her head back the memory did not retreat. She rose, put on her robe, and went down to the living room. There it hung, the photograph of George's last birthday party. Illuminated prettily by the recessed light it dominated not only the living room but Brooke's life. They stood together, posed before the Martha Washington geraniums that George helped Wyatt plant the previous week. She felt the summer's heat and sensed the trickles of sweat under their clothes.

George held his hands over his mouth, stifling a giggle, the same giggle he'd stifled for the many months since they took the shot, her little boy imprisoned in a too-revealing action. Although the others in the photograph smiled, looking closely Brooke found that she didn't. Disengaged, her eyes drifted toward somewhere unknown. Of course, she was somewhere unknown then, she was in this childless future looking at a photograph of her dead child. She plucked the photograph from the wall, tucked it under her arm, and then she went out into the back yard, stood at the edge of the arroyo and stared into the blue-black night.

She walked slowly to the concrete wall and sat down. Here the real world, in every particle of dust, every piece of wood, every object shrieked its resentful, child-stealing, banshee cry at her. Looking out on the garden she spoke George's name aloud. 'Mama misses you, George,' she whispered, almost embarrassed, even if only God could hear her foolishness. Her hand sat on the ledge and she regarded her fingers. She felt a peculiar rush of blood to her head. She thought she'd spent most of her life shrunken like an emotional prune, an empty, really empty life. She desired some sort of absolution for living this fucking great empty life. And now, too late, she had a puny desire to be loved by her dead som. She stood up. Then, leaning far out over the edge, she hurled the photograph, which she had kept nestled in the crook of her arm, out toward the arroyo. It was possible she heard it crash on the rocks, she couldn't be sure.

She thought then of Emily Dickinson, her favorite poet in college, remembering these words and saying them aloud to George, without a hint now of self-consciousness:

Futile the winds
to a heart in port,
done with the compass,
done with the chart.

The phone rang and Alec answered it. When he returned, he said, "Well ...I'm glad everyone's sitting. Your sister Brooke is on her way over, so that -- according to Wyatt -- she and her brother and sister can sort things out. Her flight leaves from LAX in an hour."

"Brooke's coming here?" Kirsten asked in horror.

"Yes."

Julian leaned his head against the wall and said, with his eyes closed, "I think I'm going to throw up."

12

Today Rutger destroyed his rugby souvenirs, his programmes, his faded instruction sheets, all of them, and not page by page but in one fell swoop. He put them inside a plastic bag from Boots and then he carried them out to the wheelie-bin, put them inside and let the lid fall shut. The things were worthless. Then he rang the number for Manchester University, the old polytechnic, designed for poor boys with ambitions, arranged an interview over the phone for the course he saw advertised, which forced him to study business but would allow him access to the education course in two years, attended an interview, sat a fill-in-the-bubble examination, got offered a position on the course, went by the store and turned in his resignation to Gerald -- who, surprisingly, permited him to take his two weeks' remaining holiday time as his two weeks notice -- and then he caught a bus from Piccadilly for Didsbury.

Brooke lifted her sunglasses off her face and rested them up on the top of her head. She knelt at the headstone, one like hundreds of others, not exactly a monument to greatness, and swept her hand across the stone face, her index finger tracing his name, George Hathaway Eiffel. The stone felt already weathered. How long would it be, she wondered, before anyone visited again? Did it matter? In the wan, smoggy afternoon sunshine a scraggly Cyprus tree looked more like an afterthought than actual landscaping. A distant lawnmower clacked, but otherwise the cemetery kept its silence

'Help me,' she said, but not to anyone and not really about anything. 'Help me,' she repeated.

Even the lawnmower fell silent and the cemetery swelled with its mouldering reticence. It felt like this when you burned your bridges and the fire scorched you, but did not consume you. She bit her lower lip to stop from crying, but she really wasn't sad and she certainly wasn't angry. So painfully silent there at George's grave, the world voiceless, mute. She leaned back against the Cyprus tree and opened her eyes wide to the smoggy sky.

A bee's droning hum above her head made her feel even more detached. She looked back again to where George's flesh rotted, hidden by the dark of soil, beyond his mother's reach, in a damp place of stars and moon. Suddenly she sat up straight and leaned forward. We search always for things in the past, so that we can make the present sensible, she thought. A flowery smell blew over from another grave, swaddling her. She cried now for her baby, rivulets of tears running down her cheeks and gathering in the creases of her laugh lines. She stood up. Her tears hadn't stopped but she didn't care. Crying felt good, as good as the afterglow of a workout, a purging. She came clean. She'd waited so long to cry properly.

She walked slowly away from George's grave, she did not look back. She felt sorry not for herself but for everyone else, because she had finally learned how to cry, a feeling as profound as sex. No, better than sex, because for her sex always seemed like a forgetting and this was a remembering. She breathed deeply and wiped her nose on her arm, sniffled loudly, touched one of her little fingers to a tear. She wasn't embarrassed, she felt proud, she felt older, she who had always craved youth, and yet she felt renewed, seasoned by life, and now cherishing her wisdom of age.

She stopped in the parking lot, put her sunglasses back on, and held her face up to the sun like a flower. For a moment she nearly lost her composure, nearly shrieked and wailed. But she didn't. She clasped her arms around her chest and rocked with only a small cry of liberation. She felt free. Yes. But free of what? She whimpered. She suddenly felt as near to heaven as she would ever get. In that moment she thought she had never been more utterly herself. And yet all the time she thought this, another woman inside her brain and heart screamed:

'I just want my baby back.'

"You didn't say anything to Brooke to encourage her, did you?"

"No," Alec said curtly, "of course I didn't. I told you, I spoke with Wyatt. Brooke never came on the line."

Kirsten fanned herself with the microwave cookery book. She felt queasy in the warm kitchen. Her perfume smelled odd to her, as if it didn't mix well with her body chemistry. Something she ate or drank? She rubbed at her wrist. "What does she hope to accomplish? I don't understand."

"I suppose there'll be some putting all of the cards on the table. That sort of thing."

Kirsten loosened her bracelet and let it dangle from her fingers. When nervous or upset it always seemed to cut off her circulation. She shouldn't have worn it. Alec turned to her, and with a finger blotted away a bead of perspiration on her hairline.

"Basically it's between Brooke and Julian," Alec said. "Her visit really shouldn't worry you."
"It obviously does worry me. I doubt she'll even speak with Julian. It's all going to fall on my shoulders," she said.

Alec opened the microwave cookery book, and calmly read about button mushrooms in a mature cheddar cheese sauce. He heard and felt Kirsten fidgeting beside him. Kirsten pulled her bracelet back up on her wrist and fastened the clasp.

"I really don't feel well, Alec." She felt clammy, and yet also as if perspiration filmed her face. "Why can't I make things feel right?"
"I don't know."

"Do they feel right to you?" she asked. "Oh God. I think I'm going to throw up, right here." Once she said it her queasiness trebled. She took a deep breath and closed her eyes. She took Alec's hand and held it. On vacation once, in Hawaii, with Wyatt and Brooke and Julian, she discovered a cave, the entrance obscured by creepers. Inside, a hillside crevice lit a twenty foot grotto. Alone in the center the whistling sounds dizzied her. A cool breath of the unknown touched her, it felt like a sanctuary, a place at the same time erotic and maternal. She pulled off her clothes, lay on her back and stared up at the cloud progressions across the sky. She had a sensation of flight; she wasn't lying still at all, but thrown up and out, over Honolulu, over the Pacific. Her breath actually grew excited and she clutched the ground to stop herself from falling.

Alec said softly, "I love you, Kirsten ... I always will."

180

"I ought to strangle you," Annabella said. "Letting me find out from Pamela. That's cruel, that is."

Rutger looked back again at Gerald's closed door. "It's a good scheme, and it gives me the chance to join the education course later at Uni. And around here ... with this new Sunday opening and all ... Sunday opening's just Gerald trying to be trendy."

"I've never noticed Gerald trying to be trendy."

"I can't work a rota like this and do a degree course."

She looked at him, trying hard not to feel abandoned. For a few moments her eyes seemed unable to focus. In the end she gave up, looked at him and said, "I remember that beautiful thing you told me, that part from an American novel, about the man who said 'I know myself, but that is all.'"

"*This Side of Paradise*," he said.

She shrugged at that and then asked, "When did you decide ... about this course?"

"I can't tell you when. I just did."

"I didn't know they went looking for people who never even did 'A' levels."

He understood her upset and ignored her tone. "It's a government scheme, I had to sit one of those American style tests like, prove my brains aren't noodles."

"How'd you find about it?"

"A friend told me."

Her eyes opened wide, perhaps in anger, more likely in hurt.

"What's that for, then? You wouldn't have told me if you'd heard, would you"

She shrugged.

"I heard about it from that bloke in Obsessions ... what's his name?"

"I don't know any of those has-been ravers at Obsessions, do I?"

"You know this bloke," he said. "You introduced me to him. Albert? Albert something."

"Oh yes. Him. We dated ... once," she said, chewing a moment on one of her fingernails. A skein of hair fell out across her forehead, but she left it, a sure sign of her distress. "So you've given your two weeks, then?"

"No. I'm taking my two weeks as holiday time owing. I won't ever be coming back here, Annabella."

They looked at one another a long while.

"You gave me that card," she said.

"Nothing changes what I said in that card, so don't be daft."

"So much is happening," she said.

"Yes, but why's that make you like this?"

"Because if you imagine we'll still be friends as we were, we won't be. It never works that way."

"You've seemed to be telling me for a while now that we couldn't be friends like we were," he said.

She looked away, out a window that offered no view except the ugly flat roof of the Arndale Centre, so he knew she attempted to hide her upset. Her shoulders rose and sank quickly.

"*Annabella?*"

"I want you to love me. I want you to be the man of my dreams, not some American bloke's dreams." She turned and they looked at one another.

182

"Why can't it be that way, then? Rutger and Annabella and a big brood of children?"

"What's all this, then?"

"It's my heart, that's what it is."

He could say nothing to that and remained silent.

She chewed again on a fingernail and threw him a sideways glance. "Do I seem pitiful?"

"No," he said, "only sad. Sad isn't pitiful."

"Are you hoping to have a go with this American?"

"I might do like. One step at a time, as they say."

She took his hand and brought it close to her chest. It remained quiet. Finally, she relented and said, "That day we went to Didsbury, well I thought you were the most handsome man I'd ever seen, didn't I?"

That surprised him. "What's being handsome have to do with anything?"

"It wouldn't be so hard for me if you were ugly."

He made a face at her. "There, that's me being ugly then."

"That's you being silly," she said, "you don't know how to be ugly."

He squeezed her hand. "I can't tell you, because I don't know the words to tell you, how I appreciate what you did for me that day in Didsbury, when you made me face up to things."

"That's what friends are for, as they also say."

"Things will be all right, Annabella. For both of us. And we will be friends, better friends, friends for life."

She smiled at that, shook her head, gently kissed his cheek, and said, "No, Rutger, we won't."

"Yes, Annabella," he said resolutely, "we will."

How dare Brooke come here, how dare she intrude upon the only place which had offered him sanctuary?

His anger pinged like sonar off the Victorian conservatory's steel beams. In shafts of summer light a red-petaled flower glowed neon. He bent, sucked up the fragrance, then looking both directions along the brick path, lopped off the blossom, tucked it in his pocket and left the building. Joggers passed him as he hurried away with his talisman, beneath the chestnuts, along the edge of the meadowy parkland. His hands caressed the silky petals, the erect stamen gnarled between his fingers, the scent rose out of his jacket. He walked to the statuary doughnut in front of the old parsonage, the hole of which framed St. James' church tower. There, he pulled the flower from his pocket and pressed it against his face. The scent filled him and his sudden anger jolted him like Frankenstein on the slab.

He breathed and breathed and ran the petals over his lips.

"We're trying to take a photograph."

He turned to look at an elderly couple, cameras in hand. They gestured toward the doughnut.

"Do you mind?" the woman pursued testily.

He hurled the remnants of flower up into the air and watched them drop into the dry basin of the fountain. Alec's bike, which he had borrowed, rested against the old parsonage and he went toward it. But, in the crosswalk, sunlight filled his eyes. When he closed them he still smelled the flower, and his focus-less anger stalked him, stalked him until finally it surrounded him in its aura. Somewhere, far away, he heard a car horn honk, but only gently against his anger and the smell of the flower. George, he thought, George, I'm so goddamned sorry for turning my back on you. *So goddamned sorry, kiddo.*

He ran to Alec's bike, unlocked it, climbed on it and pedaled furiously in and out of traffic, all the way to the house. At the front door he simply tossed the bike aside, didn't hear it bang against the fender of Kirsten's parked car, didn't care, didn't look. He rushed through the front door and up the stairs. Alec had left the stereo on in the small bedroom he called his 'office,' it throbbed sexually. Julian flew into the room, pulled the stereo out of the bookcase, and dashed it against the floor. The house fell quiet then.

He lifted his foot and kicked at Alec's desk, papers flew up against the wall and drifted down behind the bookcase. Sweat beaded on Julian's upper lip. When he went into his own room and sat down a moment, Kirsten's cat looked up at him quizzically, from where she nestled on the duvet, and mewed. Julian hurled a stuffed pillow at her. When it struck her she leapt straight up off the bed like a springbok and pronked, caterwauling, down the hallway.

Then Julian took his clothes off and stood naked at the window. He pushed the drapes back as far as they would go and watched as a starling flitted down to the window ledge, observing him as he observed it. Across the street the vacuum faces of other houses glowered back at him. His eyes stung, fiery from emotion and the moisturizer he'd rubbed on the brown swathes beneath his eyes. The starling peeped.

A car horn sounded in the street and the bird disappeared, up toward the tree, into branches. At Mrs. Jackson's first floor balcony her visiting daughter came out to shake a rug, and ended up gossiping to a handsome plumber with tortoise shell glasses, working at Number 14. Julian watched the rug drag along the balcony floor as the woman talked. Then the woman straightened, gave the cloth a cursory flap, and went back inside. Julian opened the window and stepped out on the window ledge. The sun felt warm on his chest. He liked it, it seemed quite natural. He looked down. But the handsome plumber had gone away, the street looked deserted. Birds sang in the chestnut tree, and his blood pulsed audibly in his arteries, like music, the music of his own life, metronomic blood pulsing. A wave against the shore, the world's sensations pushed against him.

What did George look for anyway, out on that breakwater? It wasn't like him to wander away. What had he said in the car on the way down? Something about seashells, something about having told his mama and daddy that he'd look for seashells. That was it. George looked for shells. And, of course, there were barnacles on the breakwater which, to a five year old, must have looked like seashells ripe for harvest.

Rutger came suddenly around the corner of the neighbor's house, from the direction of the bus stop. He looked up through the chestnut tree and stopped in his tracks. Julian waved calmly at him, friendly, reassuringly perhaps.

"Do you like Virginia Woolf?" he shouted down from on high.

Rutger stood frozen, silent.

"'And in me too the wave rises,'" Julian quoted, perfectly, from the planned reading he and

186

some friends did for graduation fifteen years before, "It swells; it arches its back. I am aware once more of a new desire, something rising beneath me like the proud horse whose rider first spurs and then pulls him back. What enemy do we now perceive advancing against us, you whom I ride now, as we stand pawing this stretch of pavement? It is death. Death is the enemy. It is death against whom I ride with my spear couched and my hair flying back like a young man's, like Percival's, when he galloped in India. I strike spurs into my horse. Against you I will fling myself, unvanquished and unyielding, O Death!'

Seashells.

He waved again at Rutger.

Then he jumped.

"He doesn't want to see you," Rutger said.

"He said so?" Kirsten asked.

"He can't talk, but he shook his head."

"Is he allowed to decide that?" Alec asked.

"Why not?"

"This is a hospital," Kirsten said, "I mean, can a patient decide not to see someone? A family member?"

"Of course," Rutger said. "It's his right."

"That seems wrong, that doesn't seem like a right someone should have," Alec said.

"Why's that, then?"

"Good grief." Kirsten sat down on one of the hard plastic chairs. "I wonder why he won't see us?"

"Would you `want to see him, if you were lying in the bed?" Alec asked.

She considered that. "Maybe not."

"You see."

"But I'm not the one who --"

"Kirsten," Alec said, cutting her off with a look at Rutger.

But Kirsten continued, "We're the ones who've got the right to be pissed off, he's no right to have any argument with us at all. I'm really sick of this, sick of it." Her color had come up and her cheeks sizzled angrily. She and Alec stared at one another for a moment, then Alec shrugged and he too sat down. They were all silent. A nurse bustled by the hallway. A gruff announcement came over the intercom, television sounds echoed from a lounge. A man read a morning paper next to the elevator, his unshaven face worn out.

"Were you there?" Alec asked Rutger.

"I was just arriving, I was in the street."

"That must have been difficult for you."

"Yes." He lowered his head into his hands, waited a moment, then looked up again. "Yes, it was."

"Look," Kirsten challenged, "why won't he see us?"

"I think he doesn't respect the way you've treated him over his nephew's death," Rutger said. "In the ambulance he said something about seashells, and that ... was his name George, the nephew?"

"Yes."

"That George was looking for shells and ... Brooke?"

"My sister," Kirsten said, "George's mother."

"That Brooke has known about it all along. He saw barnacles, I think Julian said, on the breakwater.

At any rate, there's a big distance like," Rutger told her, "between Julian and his loved ones."

"I know that, I'm presumably one of his 'loved ones.' And just who are you, by the way?" Kirsten asked, emphasizing the fact that Rutger might not be considered a 'loved one.'

"My name's Rutger. I'm Julian's boyfriend."

"*Boyfriend?*"

Rutger met her eyes and, with difficulty, stared back at her until she flinched and looked away. "Boyfriend," he said curtly.

"Well, whatever you are, you seem to know a lot about things like distance between Julian and his family."

"I know what Julian has told me, and to be honest with you, I think this distance from his family is one of the reasons why he jumped." Rutger's voice cracked and he too glanced away, down the corridor.

Alec cradled Kirsten's face a moment in his hands. "We mustn't overreact."

She pushed him away. "Whatever." Then she looked at Rutger. "How is he?"

"In and out of consciousness. Quite bad."

"Is he going to die?" Kirsten asked, and immediately she reflected on why she hadn't worded her sentence as 'is he going to live?'

"I think they believe he'll live," Rutger said, and he wished he had enough nerve to add, 'sorry to disappoint you.' "However, he's not at all well. There's something internal and there's something ... spinal. And his right leg's broken." He looked vague. "I'm afraid I didn't listen to all of it. I'm not a doctor, am I? But he suffered no brain injury."

"I think I'll go ahead and go in," Kirsten said. "From the sound of things how will he even know I'm there? Can he see?"

"When his eyes are open," Rutger said inanely, and then to cover his embarrassment at his remark he said, "I mean, most often they're closed, that's what I mean."

Kirsten stood up. "Then I'm going in."

"But he doesn't want it," Rutger reiterated.

"Too damn bad. If he wanted to make the rules he shouldn't have jumped out of my goddamned window."

She walked the ten feet to the door, opened it, and stepped inside. Three patients shared the room. Monitors. A strange bleeping noise. Darkened window. Julian's bed stood closest to the door and with his closed bruised eyes he looked barely recognizable, his face swollen and purplish. A gash ran down the side of his face and sutures speckled his lower lip, his head partly shaved and a large bandage like a hat applied to the right side. One arm lay outside the covers, with tubes running into it, the other hidden beneath the sheet. Kirsten walked up close to the bed. An antiseptic effluvium greeted her. She looked down on her brother a long while, watched him breathe evenly, asleep. A machine flickered behind him. One of the other patients mumbled something groggily, but she didn't even look. She left the room.

Alec and Rutger were where she left them, but engrossed now in conversation. Hearing her they looked up.

"Is he sleeping?" Rutger asked.

"Yes."

"You can see how ill he is, then."

"I can see." She sat down again next to Alec. "Shouldn't I talk to the doctor or something? See what the prognosis is, something like that?"

Alec hunched his shoulders and said nothing.

"How can I find his doctor?"

"Down there," Rutger gestured. "The nursing station, they can tell you."

"Want me to come with you?" Alec asked her.

"No." She stood up and went down the hall, in the direction Rutger indicated.

At the nursing station a woman looked up at her from over a stack of forms, inquiring what she wanted with the merest raise of an eyebrow. Kirsten asked in her strongest American accent to see Julian's doctor, explaining her status as sister. The nurse eyed her a moment, decided she mattered, then motioned her to a seat on a vinyl-covered couch. She disappeared into a room behind the station. Minutes crept by. Down at the end of the corridor Kirsten could still see Alec and Rutger. The nurse had not come back. A family with a child paced up and down the hallway, speaking alternately in English and in what Kirsten imagined to be Romanian. The door opened and a woman in a green smock burst through.

"You're his sister?" she asked, coming around the counter to Kirsten.

Kirsten stood up. "Yes."

They shook hands.

"Your brother is not at all well."

"What's the prognosis?" Kirsten asked.

The doctor looked momentarily surprised by the directness then said, "There's some damage to his heart, from the blow. We've been worried about an infarct. I think there might be a need to bring in a specialist for his back. A hair-line fracture perhaps, nerve damage, I can't be sure. It's not my specialty. "

"What I guess I mean is whether he's going to live or not."

"I think so. It's most likely."

"He doesn't want to see me," Kirsten said.

191

The doctor looked down at the ground a moment. "You've been made aware that this was a suicide attempt?"

"Yes. It was my guest room window he jumped out. Our house stands a bit high on the hill, above the street."

"I'm sorry," the doctor said.

"Do you think I should stay?"

The doctor looked disconcerted. "That's not for me to have an opinion, is it?"

"No. I suppose it isn't."

"I think he will live."

"All right," Kirsten said.

13

Kirsten started back down the hall toward Rutger and Alec. But she stopped in the corridor midway. A white-hot arc of light shot across her eyes, she heard the crack, smelled the sulfur. She blinked, like being in the middle of one of those dreams where you try to run but can't, a dream of paralysis. She gaped. Motionless. A seizure? Another white-hot arc of light shot across her eyes. Once more she blinked it away. Her hands fell to her side and she simply stood there. The world flowed around her and then it flowed away, she watched it bump against her -- the real world of desires, place, future, past, hopes, fears -- and then it sped off. Alec and Rutger grew hazy, figures in an impressionist painting. Was she going to faint? She blinked yet again.

Things once more grew distinct. But still she couldn't move, still she stood in the corridor and waited. Waited for what? For this, she realized, all at once. The water cleared and she saw to the bottom. She discovered the truth. She must decide who she was not before she could determine who she was. That was it, of course, and what she waited for was this significant act. And so she did it, did it precisely because she waited for it, because it signified, because it spoke the truth in a voice even the deafest listener could hear.

She left. Emotionally first. She let go. She let it all go. And then, physically, she acted out the very same impulse. She made it complete. She dotted i's and crossed t's. With a nod in Alec's direction -- who finally seemed to have noticed that something had gone wrong -- she turned. Finding, in fact, that she really could move she went to the lift, pressed the button, rode down to the lobby, walked through the lobby, went out the automatic doors, and then out to the bus stop. She never looked back, not even once, not even for a glimpse, didn't even feel the presence of the hospital, as if where once a building stood now nothing at all remained, just a black hole, an extraordinary nothingness.

At precisely that moment Kirsten and her baby started life afresh.

Julian looked up and saw Rutger staring at him.

"You looked deep in thought," Rutger said.

"I was thinking I've got a past now," Julian said, in a muffled cottony voice, "like wearing a scarlet letter, murder and attempted suicide. Women and babies will cross to the other side of the street, I won't cast a shadow, I'll make old ladies in supermarkets spontaneously combust, people will hold up crucifixes to scare me away."

Rutger closed his eyes a moment, and while they were closed said, "'After a storm, comes a calm.' One of my dad's sayings."

"Is this the calm?" Julian asked.

"I think it might still be the last of the storm, don't you?"

"Yes."

They were silent a while.

"Are you really going to university?" Julian asked.

"Yes."

"How come?"

"It's basically about the way we live our lives, I suppose you'd say, about how we just don't fit into the straight world like, and how maybe we've got to come up with something new. I'm going to be the best gay teacher this country's ever seen."

"And there have been some screamers."

"No doubt."

"How come you've hidden your light under a bushel all these years?"

"No answer for that," Rutger said. "I once told my friend Annabella that I was 'a tribute to failed ambition.' But it was my dad's ambition for me, not my own. I didn't have any ambition, and that was the biggest problem of all. It was my dad who had big dreams for us."

"And do you have ambition now?" Julian asked.

"Yes," Rutger said. "I've changed, you know, changed incredibly. Odd. I used to think that the trouble with life was that it receded just when you thought it was in your grasp. I was always chasing the solution to life, so that I could finally be ... happy -- whatever that is -- but I decided that this receding thing meant that I'd never find the solution. But isn't 'solution' a peculiar word to use, and doesn't it just tell you a lot about me?" Rutger looked at Julian. "I'll tell you one thing. I'm not afraid anymore. And I used to be so afraid that I was nearly paralyzed."

Julian smiled at him, as best he could.

Rutger smiled back.

The man in the next bed snored loudly.

Rutger pulled back the sheet and kissed the pocket between Julian's neck and chest. "I like who you are and I even like who you've been." He glanced over his shoulder at the others in the room, saw they were sleeping and said, "Besides, look at

195

that little beast raising his bald head. Right? I mean, what man likes bashful private parts."

"And just what do you know about other men's private parts?"

"Obviously," he told Julian, "more than you think."

The intensity of their hell-raising punitive passion frightened Wyatt. Their love-making now left him completely shattered. Brooke would not be kept through sex, he knew that, but he had only sex left to him. He had worked at being good in bed, aware that often he disappointed her. Now his efforts were doubled, trebled perhaps. He gently stroked her hair and felt himself grow hard again, as if he might make love to her in yet another debauched fight with his son's ghost for ownership of this wife and mother.

But she turned her face to him and said, "What the fuck's with you?"

"I love you."

"I know that, I meant ..."

"Can't you say you love me too?" he begged.

He needed to hear it. Wyatt had never been more in need of love. And Brooke's inability to provide it proved just as strong as his need for it.

"Why do I have to keep saying it?" she asked. "I have said it. I say it constantly."

"So say it now, say it again."

"No," she steamed. Her eyes were suddenly unrecognizable to him. "I won't say it on command."

"But you do love me?" Someone else asked this, someone over whom Wyatt had no control.

"*Oh, for fuck's sake.*" She pulled away from him and stood up, wonderfully naked, angry. "I've got exactly an hour and half until check in. You know how they are now with international flights, frigging terrorists and every other damn riff-raff."

"It takes twenty minutes to get to LAX."

"Half an hour is what it takes, Wyatt, and I want to try and change my seat."

She went into the bathroom. The shower ran. Wyatt lay on his back and thought about things. Then he climbed from bed and joined her in the shower. Cradled beneath the water he thought maybe she did love him again. Her lips were the lips which had kissed him before. He traced a waterfall line of love down her body. She curled the hair on his chest with her fingers, as always. They leaned into the corner and she climbed upon him. He thundered explosively against and within her. She sighed. If not love, Wyatt could hope to get no closer. They came together, thrashed like caught fish against the tiles. She rested her head against his neck and her breath, when he turned off the shower head, felt coolish-hot against his skin.

He wanted not to say it, but he did. "I love you."

She looked up him, her eyes bright from sex. "I love you, too," she said, imprisoned, without a choice. Tiny flames of resentment shone in her eyes. I've got to get going," she announced.

The spell broke. He opened the door, handed her a towel, and toweled himself dry. They dressed quickly, separately, thoughtfully. When he turned to her she wore a pink and blue blouse and skirt. He ached for her, wanted her to love him.

"You've missed a belt loop," she said.

"Belt loops are the least of my concerns."

She looked through him. "Leave it, then, I'm late anyway."

He took her in his arm and held on to her.

"Wyatt," she shrieked.

"What?

"Leave me alone."

"*Brooke.*"

"Don't raise your voice to me," she threatened.

"It's just that I'm ... in need or something."

"You're in need, fine, but I'm going to miss my plane," she said coldly. "Listen," she added, having embarrassed herself with that remark and wanting to appear more rational. "You need to go back to the center again, you need to see someone. You need help."

"You can dismiss me that simply?"

"I'm not dismissing you," she said, "I'm trying to help you." She began her move toward the door. "You're obsessive."

"I'm not either. I just want you to love me, that's all."

She turned away from him at that and started down the stairs.

"Brooke?"

She looked up at him from the bottom of the stairwell and her eyes were spotlit, he thought she looked like a go-go dancer or something. He descended the stairs behind and her and opened the door. With a pterodactyl scream the garage door opened. He put her suitcase in the trunk, opened her door and got in himself. They were silent. The engine roared as they flew down 405. Dusk dripped over the freeway, headlights appeared like flickering lamps in misty murk. Only the radio spoke into the silence.

As they rocketed along Sepulveda Boulevard, on the approach to the airport, she said sharply, "just drop me off."

"I'm coming in."

"Why?" she asked. "I've only got a few minutes."

"Aren't you sad?"

"Sad?"

"About leaving me? I want you to be sad because you're leaving me behind," he said.

"Oh, for the love of God, just piss off, Wyatt," she glowered.

He pulled up in front of the American Airlines sign and popped the trunk. She barely touched his arm as she climbed out. He watched her in the rearview mirror. She took out her suitcase. But she came back to the car and he rolled down his window.

"Look. I"ll call you when I get to Kirsten's." She bent and kissed his lips, a concession.

"I love you," he said.

Outwardly, in times of crisis, Wyatt appeared unchanged. Unlike Brooke, he never exploded. He maintained equilibrium. Although he knew therapists considered crying to be a feel-good thing, Wyatt didn't cry. He shed not a tear for two months after George died; and when finally he did cry, he did so secretively, twice in the car and once in the garage. He didn't want to pursue these thoughts. Instead he heaved the weights one final time, felt the thready pull against his muscles, savored the tensile rage of sinew and blood. Then he plunked them down and sat up. Sweat glistened on his chest. Light headed, he stood up and leaned against the railing along the window.

His stomach muscles danced of their own accord, then tautly came together again. He looked around the gym floor at the mostly mid-thirties professionals, vaguely good bodies and receding hairlines, men horny for a real fuck after years of married hum-drum, men watching each other watch each other as if that made all this play-acting less than pitiable.

Wyatt breathed deeply and closed his eyes. His body felt controlled. Why couldn't the rest of his life feel that way? He poked around on his chest, touching beadlets of sweat, then bringing his own salty taste up to his lips. He liked this taste, a kind of continuity, a remembrance of a Honolulu motel room, where Brooke licked the sweat off his chest and then touched her tongue to his. Such a wild, salty tingle, like an electrode sizzling from contact with water. How did the poem go? 'They flee from me that sometime did me seek?' Wyatt spent his young adulthood fighting Brooke off, she wanted him that much, hungering for his body with real desire. And now? Now she hungered only for revenge, in England, far away from him physically, far away from him emotionally.

He went through to the shower and curled his body up beneath the spray. When finished, he dressed slowly. In front of the mirror he primped too long over his hair, blow-dried it, combed it, then he went out to the lobby, got a candy bar from the machine, and ate it quietly next to a sickly-looking ficus tree. It made him sad, that long-neglected ficus, like the ones you see for sale in discount stores, dessicated memories of some distant jungle.

Music thump-thumped from an aerobics class. People came and went through the doors. Wyatt took his wallet from his back pocket, consulted a little phone company calling card, and walked over to the pay phone. His palms sweated, like asking someone out on a date; his throat felt tight. He knew Brooke couldn't possibly be at home ... but she might be, she might have changed her mind and returned unexpectedly, missed him so much she couldn't be apart from him and fled home again from the airport in tears. That did not in the least sound like Brooke, but it was possible.

Wasn't it?

He dialed the numbers and waited. But the voicemail answered. 'Hi, you've reached the Eiffels. Neither Wyatt nor Brooke can come to the phone. right now If you'd like to leave a message, please do so when you hear the tone.' Wyatt heard the tone, but he hung up. If he left a message he'd just have to erase it himself in twenty minutes. He wouldn't do that. It seemed comical. Enough, somehow, to have heard Brooke's voice. He crumpled up the candy wrapper and plunged out into the sunshine.

He stood in the entrance, miserable within his warm muscles. A pair of women, late twenties perhaps, come toward the door. He grew aware of them even as far away as the bank. They approached him and he suddenly saw them become aware of him too, their eyes on his thick head of hair, his puppy-dog eyes, his well-shaped chest, his strong arms. Their eyes burned him like lasers. Around the pretty blonde's wrist was an expensive bangle, definitely a man's gift. But the sexy brunette wore neither ring nor bracelet. Available, Wyatt thought, and for a moment his hormonal howl at this available woman obliterated even the pain of George's death and the dismay of Brooke's departure. For a moment he felt completely alive again.

The woman smiled. Wyatt smiled back. But he let them walk past him into the club. Of what interest could the woman be to him, he thought, when he already had the woman of his dreams, the mother of his child, the woman with whom he had slept for the last ten years.

Brooke, his heart cried, *Brooke*.

And he recognized himself as Wyatt Eiffel again, and no longer felt alive.

The heat struck Julian like a blow to the chest and he shielded his eyes. Though he knew he lay in bed in the Manchester Royal Infirmary, he also knew he stood in the open air in Los Angeles, arms crossed on his chest, broiled by the sun. Behind his imagined sunglasses his eyes nearly closed, looking at nothing in particular, and for a long while he felt only the physical sensations of heat, sweat, and thirst. Then his hands tore open the screen door to his mother's kitchen and he ran into the house with every fiber of his soul steaming.

The gray faces of household appliances taunted him. His mother, in a terry cloth robe and plastic sleeping cap, said, "Hh, God, it's just you, honey. I thought I heard somebody out there."

"Only me." His urge to smash singed his heart, but he said not unkindly, "it's a beautiful morning."

"Have a glass of milk."

"Thanks." He sensed his eyes glow red with some demonic need for reality, for now.

Milk flooded the two-handled plastic mug, the one George used as a baby. Julian often gave him drinks from this mug. Little teeth marks chomped along all along the plastic drinking spout. The milk foamed, frothed, deceived with memories. The kitchen's fluorescent lights brought out the milk's iridescence, brought out the truth.

"Anyway," he said, "I'm sorry if I woke you up."

"Oh, hell, dad's been snoring like a Mack Truck lately. I wouldn't know what a good night's sleep is. There's a great looking recipe for summer fudge brownies in the Good Housekeeping. I may as well whip up a batch, you kids are eating like rodents these days."

The house, his parents' house, settled around him. He felt it smother the flames of his passion. "I think the vessel, that with fugitive Articulation answer'd, Once did live, And merry make; and the cold lip I kiss'd, How many kisses might it take -- and give!' *The Rubaiyat.* Fitzgerald's adaptation. 'There was the Door to which I found no key; There was the Veil through which I might not see: Some little talk of ME and THEE there was -- And then no more of THEE and ME.'"

"You're a murdering asshole, darling," his mother told him, her glasses fogging with the steam which rose off Julian's skin. She placed a hand against his burning cheek. "Damned to Hell."

Then, as if from out of his mother's fingers on his face, he became aware of his bed, his surroundings, the sounds of the hospital and yet once again he was back in California, where the afternoon heat occluded thought. An effort to keep his eyes from closing against the dust of the waning day, the clasp on his watch band glinted meanly as he waved at other teachers, the smoky cologne which that morning smelled sexy now resembled one of his grandmother's pomanders. Parking lot goodbyes sounded more like sighs, shirt, socks, underwear, sweaty. The new bank building, the fast-food restaurant across the street, the wide, straight road flanked by palm trees, all just dusty with the numbing heat.

Everyone, in their torpid goodbyes, their many languid eyes, anticipated the cool, odorous night. Doors slammed, engines started, air-conditioners and radios punched on. Exhaust and dust mingled, sun refracted off glass, white daisies rocked lazily in the flower beds, their eyes massed together and lifted to the orange-yellow sun. Julian flicked the material of his sshirt, drove to the stop sign, and waited for cross traffic, aiming the air-conditioning vents at his perspiring face.

Though his thick hair irritated him, already the cold air restored his temper. In his rearview mirror he saw the school, the shopping center, disjointed parts of this disjointed suburb, and he felt happy. He turned the radio up, loosening his tie and undoing the top buttons of his shirt. Los Angeles wit poured forth from the radio, he traveled in an insulated cocoon, a time traveler past the items of his youth: long-rusting tin cans, broken irrigation pipes, mail boxes.

"I like to hear crickets singing at night," he said to George, who sat next to him on the front seat.

"What else do you like?" George asked.

"Honeysuckle blossoms, morning clouds of dust in the car window, the sounds of a water pump, barking dogs chasing skinny rabbits."

"But I'll never see any of those things," George said and then he floated up and out the car window, winding his way up into a cloudless sky, until he was merely a pinpoint on the horizon ...

"There's some tea and toast," a nurse told Julian. "Oh and I've turned down that bloody radiator, keeps it hot as the tropics in here if I don't watch out."

Julian turned his head slightly, the better to see the man's face. "Thanks."

"Feeling better?"

"Feeling weird."

The nurse smiled. "People pay good money on Saturday night to feel weird and thus better."

"But it comes at a cost," Julian said, inclining his head toward the painkiller in the nurse's hand.

"Tell me about it," the man said. "Now, show me your arm."

Kirsten pulled on her robe and went to the window, where moonlight poured through open curtains. Down below, beside the pond, she saw Alec's outline. For a long while she watched his silent silhouette, then she went downstairs and out over the grass to him.

"Hi," he said, as she approached.

"Hi." She sat on the ground beside him, hand on his foot, "I saw you down here all alone. I had mom and dad on the phone earlier, you know, filling them in on Julian. They send their regards."

"Still puzzling over why I rang them with news about the baby?"

"I don't think they've puzzled over that at all," Kirsten said. "I'm the one who was angry about it; mom and dad wouldn't know the difference."

"Accept my apologies?"

She turned her face toward him. "I suppose I already have, haven't I?"

They listened to the sucking of the pond's filter and a distant squeal of brakes on the Kingsway. Alec leaned his head back and opened his eyes to the stars. "I've never felt like this. Never."

"Like what?" she asked.

"I'm not sure I can put words to it." But then he said, "As if I wanted to run away."

"Perhaps you should then," she said.

"Well, it's only a frame of mind. Maybe the feeling's just one of nothingness, but that sounds hackneyed."

"And you don't like sounding ... hackneyed," she said, reluctant to use a word she only barely understood.

"I don't like quite a few of the things I do and feel."

"Such as?"

"Oh, I don't know. My inability to accept myself."

She looked up. The night hid his face, but beyond his head, like halos, were stars and moon. She recalled a time when she rarely looked at the sky ... now it was a preoccupation. "It's hard to accept yourself. Remember I once asked you why I knew I was a beautiful woman, but was continually afraid that I was unattractive? I've never been able to accept myself for who I really am. Funny that, isn't it?" She touched him and said, "I know it's been hard for you, Alec."

"You know what's been hard for me?" he asked.

"Growing older."

"I wonder what the rest of my life will be like? I've been really rather frightened down here considering that."

"I understand," she said softly.

"Have you fallen out of love with me?" he asked her.

The question caught her unprepared. "No ... not at all. I tried it once with someone else," she stumbled, "years and years ago, but without you ... it was just all wrong."

"Tried it?"

"Tried it," she said. After a pause she continued, "Of course I still love you."

"You worry me."

"Why?"

"I don't know. I've always felt flattered that you share so much with me."

"It's what comes from marrying an American, I suppose. If I didn't share my feelings with you I'd probably share them with the clerk at Sainsbury's. Besides, I'm married to this man who once said to me, 'with all that dark hair, you make me believe that one woman at least walks in beauty like the night.'"

"I remember when I said it. I wanted to get you into bed."

"It worked," she said.

"It worked," he agreed.

They both laughed.

Kirsten regarded him. "Alec, just why are you out here feeling sorry for yourself?"

"It's not only myself. Tonight I also feel sorry for Julian, and for you too, I suppose. Come to think of it, I feel sorry for the whole damn world tonight."

"You needn't feel sorry for me," she said. "Truth be told, I've never felt more hopeful." Her eyes closed as she thought. "*Il y a bien du monde aujourd'hui a Versailles*," she muttered dreamily.

"What?"

"It's something that always comes to me. I've no idea where I learned it. Mr. Blasingame's history class in high school, I think, sophomore year. It's one of those things that rattles around in your head all your life. Don't you have those sorts of things?"

"Yes," he said, "but not in French."

"I think it was what Marie Antoinette said, when Louis XV forced her to apologize for shunning Madame du Barry. Mr. Blasingame told us it meant something like 'everyone and his dog is here at Versailles today,' which I always think is sad, even if you're not supposed to feel sorry for Marie Antoinette."

"I saw her shoes," Alec said. "Somewhere. Fontainebleu maybe? Empress Eugenie used to wear them around for a ho-ho. You know, Napoleon III's ..."

"I know who Eugenie was," she said, looking at him. She strengthened her grip around him a moment. "We really don't have it so bad, Alec, do we? I mean, we're pretty lucky compared to most." She smiled, reached up, took his hand.

He kissed her forehead.

"Do you remember the dream I had, with George all grown up?"

"Yes."

"I'm not sure I told you the whole truth about it. I think it was you and George both, together I mean. I think George had your face, but I didn't want to tell you, I kept it secret. I can't say why."

Alec was hushed.

"And now I've told you," she said.

Her teeth grabbed a clump of her own hair. She liked the sound of that crisp crunch, it made her feel seventeen years old again. She sat through every high school class chewing bovinely on her hair. "If I were to write a novel now, you know, not that I'm going to for God's sake, I think my characters would make love just right. I mean, all of my sex scenes, they'd be, well ... appropriate for the characters."

"This is a consequential thought?"

"Very."

"Then I guess we understand one another, Kirsten."

Alec stood up straight, his body still that of a young man, hard, well-formed, broad-shouldered. He blinked away the heady fragrances of so many memories and stepped to the edge of the pond. He thought of Kirsten and their baby and their home, he thought of being together. His voice came back on the breeze.

"I tried to throw that robe away, you know."

"I know," she said. "I fetched it out of the wheelie bin."

"I love you, Kirsten. You know ... I'll always love you."

14

Brooke saw Alec first and called out his name. He came forward and they embraced just outside the metal barrier.

"Hello, Chris," he said.

"Hi."

"May I?" he asked, as he picked up her carry-on bag. Then he gestured in the direction of the car park. "Good flight?"

She shrugged. "I don't know how people actually sleep on planes."

"Nor I," he said.

"Mom and dad send their best, and Wyatt, of course."

"How is he?"

"Better," she said.

He felt momentarily awkward, remembering his phone call about the baby, and then how Brooke must feel about Kirsten's child. Conflicting emotions tumbled around in him before he could say, "That's good. We're this way."

They walked quietly. She looked surprisingly perky to him, her make-up fresh, her summery blouse and skirt fashionable. She'd obviously put on perfume before they landed. He'd expected a haggard-looking crone, but in many ways Brooke had never looked better.

"I suppose you're wondering why I've come?" she asked.

"Wyatt said you had to sort things out with Kirsten and Julian."

"Yes. That's true."

"Is there another reason?" he asked.

"Oh, Alec, I'm just like some piece of ... what? Flotsam and jetsam? Driftwood? I got the idea into my head that I should come over here and have it all out."

"Have what out?"

"Be with Kirsten, then," she said, ignoring his question, "and here I am. You don't mind, do you?"

"Perhaps, yes, a bit."

She looked stunned, then she looked away. Time passed. She stopped walking and, turning to him, her eyes ripped through him. He glanced away, frightened perhaps.

"*Shit*," she said.

"You asked."

"I don't think I meant it seriously," she said.

"Brooke," Alec said, his calmness entirely a ruse, "Julian has tried to kill himself."

She stood unmoving in front of a large window. For a very brief moment it seemed that she smiled. Then, shaking her head, she said quietly, "I see."

"He jumped from one of our windows, he's still in hospital and will be for weeks, battered, bruised and lucky to be alive, but alive nonetheless."

"I see," she repeated.

Alec looked at her, but she turned away again, hiding her face from his scrutiny.

"You coming here now does rather complicate things," he said.

"I can understand that."

"However, we'll make it work. Don't worry."

Again they walked silently.

Then she stopped, touched his arm, and said, "if he really meant to kill himself, he would have."

Alec said nothing.

"Don't you agree?"

"I'm not able to say. I'm sure he nearly *did* kill himself."

"It was drama."

Again he pointed toward the sign for the car park, and again they walked.

"I suppose it was rather dramatic. A show. Now he's got our attention focused on him there in his hospital bed. Think about it. Julian has pulled a fast one," she said venomously. "He's stolen George's thunder."

Gooseflesh crawled up Alec's arms. She looked now like a hard-hearted reptile, wiping her mouth as if venom dribbled from her fangs down her chin. However, he knew she was still a grieving mother and needed to be given allowance. How long did you give someone an allowance like that?

"We're down this walkway," he said, "and up the lift."

She followed him.

"Beautiful morning," he told her, "bags of welcome sunshine."

She looked out the windows which lined the corridor. "Does he know I'm coming?"

Alec refused to say anything more about Julian. As they came up to the lift he pressed the button and said, "You haven't seen my new car, have you?"

She eyeballed him. "No," she said softly, but with a remaining taste of venom, "I haven't, Alec."

Rutger hurried down the gravel path toward the main buildings of Manchester Royal Infirmary. Beneath morning mist, the plants bordering the staff car park were encased in dew. Birds chirped incongruously in a hedge. Here it seemed neither urban nor hospital-like. As he came around the corner he nearly collided head-on with Alec.

They stopped and looked at each other.

"Hello," Rutger said.

"Morning," Alec said.

"Long night?" Rutger asked.

"Too short, actually. Why do you ask?"

"Because you look tired," Rutger told him.

"I am." Alec looked over the hospital grounds. "'It's 1913 and Edwardian England is about to vanish into history.'"

"*Pardon me?*"

"It's on the front of the Penguin edition of *The Shooting Party*. One of my favorite books ... our favorite books actually. Kirsten and I both love that book, and the film. With James Mason?"

"I don't know it."

"Comes from lecturing on English literature, I suppose. Well, that's what this whole thing is, Rutger. I feel like the world I know is about to vanish into history, as if I've fallen through a tunnel, like Alice. Maybe the white rabbit'll come running by any minute."

"Maybe he's waiting up in Julian's room."

"Know what I mean, then? This thing that's happened to Julian, it isn't the real world at all. This is something else, something where a person you care about is lost and unable to live."

"Do you care about Julian?" Rutger asked.

Alec seemed reluctant to answer at first. Then he looked Rutger in the face and said, "When George died, it turned a light on, and everything was either visible or else throwing a shadow."

"Julian misses his family, you know, misses their ... presence, like, in his life," Rutger said.

Alec looked at him. "I suppose, in many ways, we've let him know we blame him."

"He knows that you blame him."

"I'm sure," Alec said. Then he asked, "Do you love Julian?"

"It'd be too soon to say that. But yes, I think I do. Julian has helped me, more inadvertent-like than anything, to ... accept being gay. I owe him for that."

They stood quietly together, shoulder to shoulder and watched a vapory morning rise over Manchester. Housing blocks and the elevated ribbon of the Mancunian Way festooned the horizon.

"Change can be so frightening, even when it's advantageous," Alec said.

They were quiet and reflected for a moment on the frightening power of change.

Rutger remembered telling Julian that change was sanity. Was it? "Things and people do change though, don't they? It's hell if we can't accept that. So many people can't." He took Alec's hand and shook it. "I'd like to see you later."

Startled, Alec asked, "Why's that?"

"Because it's always good to talk," Rutger said. "And some day we may be family."

After a few seconds of silence Alec said, "All right. We might lunch together today, if you'd like. But, you know, it needn't have naught to do with family."

"You're right. And I'd think lunch was smashing," Rutger said, laughing at Alec's imitation Mancunian accent.

She put down the spiral binder she'd been reading and looked up, as if she knew beforehand that Brooke would appear. The brass-plated light was crooked, leaning toward her menacingly, its yellowish light smudgy. A distant humming came to her, the refrigerator perhaps, but otherwise the house seemed much too quiet. When Brooke came into the room, their eyes met unerringly, at once, and Kirsten asked, "Jet lag?"

"I thought everyone was asleep," Brooke said. Her voice had that dislocated jangle of someone whose nose detected alien smells and whose stomach needed meals in the middle of the night.

"Not me."

"What're you reading?" Brooke asked.

"It's a notebook from one of my college English classes, I found it in Alec's study when I was cleaning out the wardrobe for you. They're all my notes on Jane Austen. Funny. Until I looked through this I'd forgotten I ever read *Northanger Abbey*."

"Maybe you didn't. You know what college students are like."

"I know me," Kirsten said, "and I read everything."

"Yes, you probably did. But why do you save such things as that?"

"I really don't know. There's a bit of the pack rat in me, isn't there?" Kirsten looked away. "I don't suppose these Jane Austen notes mean a whole hell of a lot to me, if that's what you're wrinkling your nose about."

"Kirsten, stop that, of course I'm not wrinkling my nose."

One of those meaningful silences, that their mother described as 'a shoe dropping,' folded over them. They both seemed to think about the silence, and perhaps they both heard their mother's voice, because when they looked at each other it seemed their mother had joined them.

"Why've you flown over here, Chris?" Kirsten asked, uncompromisingly direct, just as her mother would.

"To be with my siblings."

"God that sounds clinical, like a tribe of ancient Germans on the west bank of the Elbe."

"Siblings is the correct word."

"'My brother and sister,' that's what most people would say, of course if you say that then you have to admit Julian's your brother. You want me to believe you really care to be with Julian, when you can't even admit he's your brother? Right."

"Why else would I have come?"

"To ensure we're being miserable?"

"Come again?"

"You don't want any of us to be doing anything but contemplating the unfairness of your life."

"How can you?"

"How can I what?" Kirsten demanded.

"Be so callous."

"I'm not callous. I've grieved for George too, cried buckets of tears. But although I can't believe I'm actually saying such a stupid thing, Brooke, life goes on."

"It doesn't," Brooke said. "It absolutely *does not* go on. It comes to a crashing halt. Period. That's what it does."

"It goes on, Chris ... it does." And Kirsten envisioned her own life going on ... on and on until her death, a string of days and nights, events, feelings, births and other deaths, and the vision both elated and scared her.

"You're wrong," Brooke said. "Any more than a car that's been totaled ever drives again

In the silence which followed her remark, she went over to Kirsten, picked up the binder, flipped it open and read a moment quietly.

"What's that?" Kirsten asked, made curious by Brooke's expression.

"'Last night I was with Alec again,'" Brooke read. "'When he made love to me, it was like nothing I'd ever even imagined. And he promises to take me camping this summer at a beach in Wales, one you can only reach by walking through a farmer's fields. And he said we'll make love there, on the beach.'" Brooke closed the binder. They looked at one another.

"How odd. I don't remember writing things like *that* in there.

"Well, it was way in the back. That must have been some love-making," Brooke said.

"It still is."

Brooke looked at her fingernails, Beirut fingernails, chewed down to the nub, nails which once were pampered darlings with a monthly manicure and were now shattered ruins, and she said, "Now you're having his baby."

"Lot of lovemaking's gone into this baby," Kirsten said.

As if less lovemaking went into George? Kirsten hadn't meant it that way, but Brooke interpreted it as a repudiation and flared, "Now you're being a bitch."

On reflection Kirsten realized she didn't care how she sounded. "So you'd be bound to say, Chris."

Once again they looked at each other, but Kirsten did not give ground. Brooke seemed to concentrate a moment on her breathing. She went to the bay window and looked out at darkness, placing one hand against the pane as if in benediction. "I want to talk about George's death. Maybe that's why I've come over. I need to talk about it."

"Haven't we already done that?"

"Have we?"

Brooke's eyes were lightless, exhaustion etched her face. She sat on the sofa and stared over the coffee table at Kirsten. Even the refrigerator went silent. Kirsten's heart softened before such misery and she regretted her coldness.

"George's gone and we have to let go of him, a large part of him, at any rate. What was, well, it just isn't anymore," Kirsten said, and to emphasize her point she tossed her notebook across the room. "We have to deal with what we've got, right here, right now." She meant her words, she meant them and she wanted to say them. Yet she felt like she burned her bridges, that saying these things was reckless.

"What have we got 'right here, right now'? I'd like to know if you can define it," Brooke said.

It hurt Kirsten then to think of Julian suffering so much that he tried to kill himself and she wished she hadn't thought, there in the hospital, that it would be better if he had succeeded. Brooke's eyes glistened now with tears and she bit her lower lip to stop from crying. There had been few times in their lives together that Kirsten had seen Brooke cry.

When Brooke spoke, her voice emerged small and thin. "I miss him."

The room suddenly filled with their thoughts of George, as if a hologram danced around them with birthday   balloons   and   ruffled   hair.

"Me too," Kirsten said.

"I feel like Julian didn't just kill George that day ... he killed me too."

"Julian didn't kill George," Kirsten said.

"So you've exonerated him?"

"It's not my place to exonerate him, because I can't, he was responsible for George and he let him ... what? Wander away. But, you know, when he was being taken to hospital this friend Rutger of his said Julian told him something about George looking for shells, and that you and Wyatt have known that all along. Have you?"

"Wyatt doesn't know what day of the week it is," Brooke snapped. Then she said, "George wanted to find us a shell."

"Then that's obviously why he went out on the breakwater."

"How can you know that?"

"Because it's obvious."

Brooke closed her eyes. When she opened them she said, "Kirsten, I'm pitiable. Without George, I don't even know who I am." A tear slid down Brooke's cheek. "I'm left behind." A painful silence smothered the conversation. Brooke stood up, walked across the room, put her hand on Kirsten's shoulder. "Looking for seashells is the sort of thing a five year old naturally does at the beach. Knowing it ... well, knowing it doesn't excuse Julian."

"But you've known it and kept it a secret and made out like everything was Julian's fault and there's more to it."

"As I say, knowing my little boy was looking for shells doesn't take away Julian's guilt."

"Julian clearly agrees with that or he wouldn't have jumped out my upstairs window on to the pavement down the hill."

An ugly silence filled the room, dispelling the George hologram. The cat stretched from her position on the sofa and extended her claws in mock battle.

"It was a bid for sympathy," Brooke spat.

"Some bid," Kirsten spat back.

"Good night, Kirsten." Brooke moved toward the doorway. "I'll see you in the morning."

"Good night," Kirsten said, and she didn't stand up.

"I should tell you," Alec said, from where he sat at the bottom of Julian's bed, "that Kirsten's been thinking about things a great deal ... and her thinking is beneficial."

"To whom?"

"Everyone," Alec said. "Kirsten is different from both you and Brooke. This morning, she was telling me about having found her old Jane Austen notes from college and what it felt like to be pregnant and for the first time in weeks, months, years maybe, she was positively radiant, all smiles."

"I think maybe the pregnancy made her smile more than the Jane Austen notes."

"She acts like she's had some unexpected victory," Alec said, "some exultation and triumph."

"Did you talk about me?"

"Of   course,"   Alec   said.

"And?"

"Kirsten loves you, but she's figured out that she ... has to get on with her life, 'get out from under the shadow of her family' is how she termed it."

"It's a long shadow."

Alec shrugged. He thought about his remark to Rutger, about George's death either lighting things up or making them throw a shadow. "Change of subject. I think Rutger's a nice man."

"He is a nice man."

"I mean nice as in ... for you ... whatever gay people say. A partner?" He obviously couldn't bring himself to use the word boyfriend. "You know."

"I doubt he wants to take on a burden like me," Julian said.

"You mustn't see yourself as a burden."

"Oh come on," Julian sighed, "I am. Everything 's somehow ... continually ... turned on its head in my life. Look at me here, in this bed, now. Think about what I've done, first George and then ... this." Quiet a moment or two, he then said, "I don't deserve Rutger."

"You'll think differently again, that's how these things go."

"Gee, thanks, coach." Acutely aware of the patients in the other beds listening to them, Julian nonetheless said, "Of course, I wouldn't have *minded* having a coach who looked like you."

They both smiled.

"What are you doing here?"

"Uni's just across Oxford Road. This gets me away from the keyboard."

"And here I thought you were playing Florence Nightingale."

"Perhaps there's a bit of that," Alec said.

"Right. You didn't even want me to come stay with you guys in the first place."

"I never said ..."

"I'm not a villain. I worry a lot about that, about making amends, putting my life back on a proper course. But I honestly can't live," he gave Alec a lost look, "with my life filled up with death. Do you forgive me. I mean, I know you loved George too."

"You aren't a villain, Julian."

"Before I went out the window, I could hardly sleep at night, thinking about George. It was like this ... mist, creeping everywhere through my life."

"All you can do is come to grips," Alec said, then he leaned forward and kissed Julian on the forehead.

His lips were warm, he smelled clean. Briefly Julian felt uncomfortable with this demonstration of affection, then he let Alec hold him and he rested the unsutured side of his face on the shoulder of Alec's sweater. He knew Alec hadn't often held anyone other than Kirsten, let alone another man, and Julian saw that it brought up something within him that he rarely if ever had experienced -- vulnerability, possession, omniscience -- but which awed him nonetheless.

Julian held out a hand to Alec's face, and put the back of it against his cheek. "Thanks."

Pulling away from Julian, Alec tried a smile. "How about a cup of tea? This is far too serious for this time of day. Rutger'll be here any minute, we don't want him to see us crying in here like a couple of old ladies, do we?"

"I hate tea. Find some coffee? Ask the frisky brown-eyed nurse named Derek, he's definitely a rule bender."

"I'll do my best."

"It's all one can ask."

Julian knew by the smell of violets that George had come into the room. Opening his eyes he saw George beside the bed, his head barely reaching above the covers.

"Hi, George."

"Hi, Uncle Julian."

"You were looking for seashells, weren't you?"

"There were some, and man they were really great ones too ... on those big rocks, only they were stuck on there *hard*."

"You were bad, George, to run away from Uncle Julian."

"I didn't run."

"You know what I mean."

"It was cold in that water and I was really scared and I was wanting to find my mama."

"I'm sorry you were cold and scared," Julian said.

"That's okay."

"You're not cold now are you?"

"No. Are you?"

"Yes. I miss you very much, George."

"You don't need to miss me, Uncle Julian."

"But I do."

"Okay then, you can."

"George, do you forgive me?" Julian asked.

"What's that mean?"

"Uncle Julian made a big mistake by not paying attention to you. He shouldn't have let you be cold and scared in that water."

"I was looking for shells," George said, "on those big rocks."

"The breakwater," Julian said.

The door opened and Rutger came into the room. "Hello," he said, looking at the other two patients, both of whom were asleep. "With whom might you be speaking?"

"George."

"Your nephew ... who drowned?"

"Yes."

Rutger sat down. "I gather he's gone now."

Julian looked at the spot where George had been standing. "Yes."

"No wonder people steal the medication you're on."

"No wonder."

"How are you feeling?" Rutger asked

"Better maybe."

Rutger looked at him directly and asked, "why did you do it? Level with me."

"I didn't do it," Julian said, "it just ... happened, like I was pushed. You know? All that lack of forgiveness, it just pushed me right out the window."

Rutger thought about that. "Rather liberating for you to conceive of it that way. Are you certain you didn't think 'I'm going to top myself and make everybody sorry they ever ran me down,' or anything like that?"

"I'm sure."

"Again interesting. My mum told me that people who commit suicide invariably have second thoughts. That's one way the police can tell it was suicide, because there's always a sign that they regret their actions. Otherwise, the authorities generally rule it was an accident."

"I didn't really fall out the window," Julian said, "so it wasn't an accident."

"But you're saying you didn't jump either."

"True."

"At the moment, Julian, my American, I feel more successful than at any time in my life, and all of it has come from right in here," he touched her chest. "Only, of course, the man I love is in the hospital after trying to kill himself."

"II swear you could drive a Smartcar down those veins of yours."

Rutger laughed. "Like 'em, do ya?"

"Do you think?

Glancing at his watch, Rutger stood up, leaned over and kissed Julian. "I love you."

Julian smiled.

Rutger went to the door, opened it and vanished.

Part Three

15

With sleeves rolled up, shirt unbuttoned, Julian stood in the farthest corner of his garden, where the oaks grew thickest and the shadows were somewhat cool. He lifted his face toward ripening fields. Julian had always suspicioned romanticizing landscape, and yet here he discovered enchantment in the mauve streaks of setting sun touching uncut hay and swollen grain; landscape as Goethe wrote it. Though the evening was advanced, the sun was reluctant to loosen its hold. The breeze embraced him. Flowers drooped in the grass, their scents flushed out by the heat. His Airedale terrier, Beowulf, only just emerged from the taxing throes of puppyhood, slept heavily beneath the apple tree. Birds fluttered overhead.

Julian looked back at Beowulf and, when he made a clicking noise, the dog leapt to his feet. Together they walked over the lawn to the patio and then into the house. Smells from his evening meal still filled his study, he caught the muffled sounds of the Mp3 playlist he'd forgotten on his computer. He picked his phone up from the chair in which he's left it and called the number.

"Hello."

"Rutger."

"My god."

"Think you'd never hear from me again?"

Breathless, Rutger said, "I gave up ... long ago."

"I thought so."

"It's what ... three years?"

"That long?"

"Yes. How are you, Julian?"

"All right. And you?"

"Okay," Rutger said quickly, "not bad."

"I suspect you've done well in college."

"I did all right like, but I packed it in, I've come back to the store with Annabella, Gerald's taken me on again."

"But why?"

After a long pause Rutger said, "I read your novel. So did the rest of the world apparently, judging from what I've seen on morning tele, though unlike me they wouldn't have seen themselves in it."

"Like it?"

"It was profound like. Annabella read it too and she thought it was brill. I loved myself, by the way."

"It may not have been you," Julian admonished. "They're making the film, I've been asked to do the first script. Weepy flicks about dying kids ... they're Hollywood's dream-come-true."

"I'm glad for you," Rutger said.

"Listen ... got any plans for the weekend?"

"No."

"Come down to my place then?" Julian asked.

"Where's 'my place?'"

"Finchampstead."

"Where's that, then?"

"Near Wokingham, Berkshire."

"London way."

"Yes."

"Well," Rutger hesitated, "I haven't got a car at the moment and there's the expense."

"Not so bad. You change in London, on the Underground from Euston, take the train from Waterloo, I'll meet you at the station in Wokingham. Simple."

Rutger stayed silent.

"How about it?" Julian pursued.

"I don't know."

"Why not?"

"Reasons. The past. Time. Water under the bridge."

"I think it's important that you come."

Rutger brightened then, sounding pleased when he asked, "When would you want me, then?"

"Come out with the commuters on Friday?"

But again Rutger hesitated. "You sound so different, don't you, Julian? Almost like a stranger."

"I'm not that, I assure you."

"All right, then." Rutger relented. "Wokingham, you say? Doesn't it just *sound* Southern. From Waterloo?"

"Yes. There's a train gets into Euston about six, I think, which puts you here by seven-thirty or so. I'll be waiting for you."

"I'll be the nervous over-dressed Mancunian," Rutger said.

Julian waved as Rutger -- wearing a bright blue shirt and beige cotton pants and carrying a small suitcase with the airline labels from a trip to Spain still attached -- came through the barrier into the lobby, the last one off the train. The other passengers had already evaporated into the suburban ether. As Rutger came toward him Julian laughed and leapt into his arms, forcing him to drop the case. They kissed necks, and then Julian picked up the suitcase and guided Rutger out to the car. Backwater peace caressed the station car park. A green oak bough bent so low it touched the roof of Julian's car.

They climbed in.

Rutger's voice sounded strained. "You look good, no, you look better than ever I've seen you. Tanned, you are."

"I shouldn't be, I know it's bad for you, but I can't seem to resist this heat wave. The Californian in me, I suppose."

"You haven't changed, Julian, not physically." Rutger tossed his hair and put on a pair of sunglasses. "Though you do have that Southern England gloss now, don't you? You've gone native. Nice car this. Pretty place Wokingham," Rutger held an uncertain hand out toward prosperous buildings. "The South always seems like a calendar picture, doesn't it?"

"Not all of it. Reading is all red brick. But wait until you see Finchampstead," Julian smiled, "that'll remind you of a calendar or two."

"That where you live?"

"Yes. I'm permanently resident here, in fact I'll take up citizenship if I'm ever able."

"But why?" Rutger wondered.

"Because England offered me sanctuary and now it's my home and I want to be here. I love the place. Nothing more complicated than that."

"You've always seemed so American to me."

"I don't reject my past," Julian said, "I'm just planning for the future."

Rutger turned away from him to look out the window. "How lucky you are." He gestured at the passing rows of trees and the gardens in front of substantial houses. An old woman pedaled by on a bicycle and across a meadow rich with buttercups cricketers were at play. "Really, it's smashing. Is it a flat you have or a house?"

"Neither," Julian smiled, "a farm."

Rutger looked at him in embarrassed surprise as Julian's success caught up with him. "I can't see you as a farmer."

Julian laughed and they chatted about the recent heat wave and then fall silent. He drove along shady Finchampstead Road out of Wokingham, past the Sandhurst Road and Nine Mile Ride, out into the summery Berkshire countryside. Rutger observed it all quietly, his window open, his hair blowing and he no longer seemed edgy, rather he seemed resigned. Julian slowed as he turned on to a gravel drive which passed beneath a leafy canopy. On one side they saw horses in a pasture, then they curved round and appeared in front of a mid-Victorian manse.

Rutger turned to him in silent approval. "You haven't told me why you rang, is it meant to be some great mystery or something?"

"It just seemed like time."

"The thought came to you ... like that?"

"You'll see. I've, well, adjusted I guess, which is the same thing as changing for me. I've been seeing a psychologist, in London, she's been helpful. In my world it seems like relationship was always synonymous with failure and pain. But now ... now I think I'm going to do better."

For a long while Julian could see nothing of Rutger's emotions, since he had turned his face away from him. Then Rutger surprised him by saying quietly, "Take me back to the station, Julian. Please?"

Julian digested this remark. "Are you serious?"

"Yes."

"How come?"

Rutger put on his sunglasses and looked away again.

"Rutger?"

"Because I wanted you. I wanted it to be us here, like this ... calling ourselves a couple."

" If you stay, Rutger, we can talk about that."

The quiet extended, folded around them.

"Will you? Please? Stay with me?"

"Forgive and forget? Happy bleeding endings and all that?"

"You're big enough to know there aren't any happy endings."

"Bloody cliches."

"True all the same," Julian suggested.

"Right you are there, mate."

"So you're angry," Julian said.

"And you're right about that too."

"So stay, Rutger. Please. I know you're upset and probably angry. And you'll think it's a cliche again, but if you didn't care, you wouldn't *be* angry. So, let's start ... well, please stay."

It remained quiet, and Julian waited until Rutger turned to him finally and nodded his head.

Julian prepared a Japanese feast and even served Sake, but their meal proved uncommunicative. After coffee Julian poured them glasses of brandy and took Rutger outside to the garden, lush with blooming flowers. But still Rutger held himself in some world of his own, aware of Julian and yet oblivious to him, his back turned so that he could stare into the fields.

"How's everyone, then?" Rutger said at last asked, turning around.

Unsure about an answer to that, as the only possible reply would be too long for the occasion, Julian merely looked at him.

"They're all well. I traveled for a couple of months with Wyatt, my brother-in-law, out in South Africa. We stayed with some lesbian chum of someone they know back in Los Angeles, in a brilliant old wooden house with a veranda and cooing birds and about a dozen fat cats and we cracked open tins of lager every night and played cards and went to art films in Cape Town. We even had a little ceremony," Julian said, "dumped out the lo mein box in the Drakensbergs."

Rutger looked baffled.

"Her mother's ashes. For some reason she had kept them in an old Chinse take-away box. Anyway, a great occasion, ashes and dried remains of fried rice."

"And your sisters?" he asked.

"We keep trying ... at least Kirsten and I do. I sent Brooke a long email at Christmas and it didn't bounce back, so I guess that's a start. Have you settled with anyone since me?" Julian asked.

"Settled? No, not settled."

"Seen anyone then?"

"You'll laugh about it, you will. It was shit-ugly. I met him in college, a nice bloke, pretty, a bit young for me maybe, I flew out to Spain with him for a fortnight. I guess it was meant to be torrid, but it was just cheap. We faught, he picked somebody else up in one of those tacky foul disco bars they have over there, full of pot-bellied Englishmen with veiny noses they've had laser-treated, complaining about the lack of talent and praying to get picked up by anything not yet using a Zimmer frame. It wasn't even worth the price of the air ticket, not to me at least. It just threw everything into relief, that's all it did." He looked at Julian for a moment and then he said, "Everything seems to have been like Alice through the Looking Glass the last years, lonely like, and barren."

"Why did you leave uni?"

Rutger only shrugged at such an unanswerable question. Then he asked Julian, "And you? Has there ... been anyone?"

"A one night stand in Edinburgh last year at the festival, another American. He's been the only one and rather unremarkable," Julian inclined his head toward Rutger, "in comparison. You know, sometimes I think I haven't even noticed the passage of time, certainly not three years."

"You've had a lot to forget, haven't you, it made it so you didn't count it all in ... what? Ordinary time."

"Perhaps that's what it is. Some things can't be explained, Rutger. I've learned that."

Their eyes met briefly, flared, then turned away.

"Like it here?" Julian asked, changing the subject.

"It's lovely, Julian, you chose well."

Julian gestured back to the house. "Come on, let's go in. It's getting chilly."

Rutger walked listlessly beside him.

"You up for an early morning hike? There are some lovely views from the top of the hill, across the Hampshire downs. When the sun's out, why it's like something Maxfield Parrish might have painted."

"Fairies and Greek columns?"

"Fluorescent color and," Julian touched his chest, "only the occasional fairy."

With his first smile that evening, Rutger looked into the distance, as if seeking fairies in tutus. "I'd like that, yes."

"A plan, then."

Julian reached out and stroked Rutger's hair, but was not surprised when Rutger moved his head away sharply.

"You need to go back to university," Julian said.

"Why's that?"

"Because you can have a great deal of happiness ahead of you, if you want it."

Rutger merely shrugged; he'd heard it all before.

"I hardly think about George's drowning anymore, not in the way I did, and yet sometimes, out of nowhere, I'll have one of those old nightmares of mine and scream out loud."

"So George's still with you."

"Yes," Julian said, "he's still with me. Although he died it's as if ... he isn't dead."

"The world's a strange place," Rutger said.

"Sometimes," Julian said, and his voice sounded far-away, musical in the way waves are musical, rhythmic and incessant, "I see the breakwater ... *that* breakwater ... stretching out in front of me, just as it was that afternoon, endless miles of geometric rock, cleaving whole villages, shopping precincts, motorways, forests, oceans ... stretching on forever, around and around and around the world."

They were speechless, absorbing this image.

"You'll always see that like," Rutger suggested.

Only birds still trilling in song broke the incipient silence of nightfall. Heavy odors of honeysuckle curled around them. They stepped up onto the terrace.

"Why'd you leave me?" Rutger asked.

Though Julian haad waited for this question, a nervous anticipatory knot unfurled itself in his stomach and as the painful knot unfurled he said in a rush, "Because ... I had to."

"Had to?" Rutger had a distant look. "You want to know the happiest moment of my life?"

"Sure."

"The first time we kissed, Julian."

"Know the happiest moment of mine? The first time I woke up and realized I hadn't dreamt about George. Come on, let's pull some chairs up and talk properly."

Then they passed through the open French doors, into the house.

Rutger awoke slowly. Sunlight dribbled across the open window's ledge. He stretched in a yawn, rose and went toward the morning. Ducks skimmed the surface of a pond. He dressed, went downstairs, found Julian had already made breakfast. When they'd eaten they went out across the garden and lawn. The sun came from behind the stable. Everything around them -- grass, trees, stones, implements -- had a rosy-gold hue. An earthy horse smell, a delicate taste of flowers, a faint disinfectant aroma scrubbed the air. Julian bore no sign of the sleepless night Rutger had endured. They watched each other as they walked and, for his part, Rutger felt as if the weekend escaped his grasp, neither his time nor his place, his mind both chilled and inflamed, an awful combination.

"You know?" Julian said, "I'm sorry I jumped out that window. It was a shitty thing to do. Selfish ... really selfish."

"I don't suppose you thought about it like that at the time." Rutger cocked his head slightly at Julian, and suddenly he felt as if a strong wind blew against him, as if he must brace himself. It felt good. "Are you happy now, Julian?"

"*Happy?*"

"Being an author? Having this farm and ... well, and all?"

"What do you think, Rutger?"

The soft way in which Julian spoke his name, the claim to past intimacy, goaded Rutger. He looked up quickly and his eyes narrowed. "Then why've you waited so long to ring me?"

"I was in a psychiatric facility in Reading for a long while. Then I was suddenly a sensation ... and how could I have known you'd care to hear from me by then."

"Don't be daft," Rutger scathed, "of course I'd want to. You didn't leave me so much as a sodding forwarding address."

Julian turned away in shame.

Tears welled up in Rutger's eyes, his sparks were that quickly extinguished. He stepped back several feet and seemed to sigh in his confusion.

"When I invited you down," Julian said, "it was because I wanted to ... how do I say it? Reach out to you? Like people did to me. Not as if you were needy, nothing like that, just --" his voice fell away. "I wanted to tell you, Rutger, that we *can* make life be what we want. Life is just like a fiction, with

239

endless possibilities for happiness as well as sadness. It's so damned relative, in the end, that it can almost be molded like clay. So ... we mold it."

Rutger reached up and grabbed a bunch of honeysuckle blossoms, which he pressed to his face. "Annabella would love it here."

"Bring her next time."

A long silence followed.

"I will," Rutger said and then he looked long at Julian. "What would it mean if I said I felt ... whole ... right now, here, with you?"

"It would mean a hell of a lot."

"But why *should* I feel it?"

Julian held out his arms, but Rutger was not yet ready for an embrace, so Julian touched Rutger's chest tentatively with both hands.

"Do you think I can still love you then?" Rutger wondered.

"I don't know."

Rutger looked again at Julian and then Julian lay his head against Rutger's chest and Rutger kissed his hair. In that simple act of affection Rutger seemed to know the truth.

"I've missed you," he said.

When Julian awoke he saw the afternoon had grown late. Sun streamed into the room and across the floor. Rutger still slept soundly. Julian got out of bed. Everything seemed somehow altered. Even putting on his underpants seemed now to have a domestic comfort in it. The still present feelings of Rutger within him were thrilling and he turned and watched Rutger breathe and he loved him.

"Julian?" Rutger asked sleepily, waking up.

He held out his hand and Julian came and sat beside him, tracing the contour of Rutger's chest with his lips and with his tongue tasting the saltiness of his skin. Rutger's arms cradled him and they sat together, that close, for several minutes. Rutger's strength brushed up against Julian and then flooded over him, and in his mind's eye he saw George's ghost retreat. Numb, and yet far too hot with sensation, Julian willed him to leave. "Go away, George," he mouthed silently.

Once Julian wept to think of losing George, whom he loved more than life itself, and now he banished him finally to that place of memory, because he wanted Rutger --- warm, alive, loving -- in his place. He put an open kiss on Rutger's mouth and took breath from him. Then he put his head snugly on Rutger's shoulder and, staring at the hair on his chest, thought, 'This is love ... this is what love feels like.' And he no longer blamed Brooke for her hatred, because if something were now to happen to Rutger – well, he too would hate whoever was responsible.

Rutger pushed Julian over backward on the bed, came to rest on his arms above him, and said, *"Love me."*